The Prince's Bride

By Yvonne Sibanda

Dedication

To the late Doctor K. C. Moonga, thank you for introducing me to self-publishing and encouraging me to never give up but continue writing. I am grateful to have met you, you were such a great man with love for God and people.

Thank you and you will forever be remembered.

Chapter 1

"NEVER ever treat any woman like this," Peggy James screamed with all the fury of a woman scorned and tried to kick the man already groaning on the ground, except this time he deflected her foot swiftly.

"You're mad lady," the man hollered back and flinched when PJ glared at him.

That made her even more furious, her mad? He was the mad one for assuming that she was a hooker and wanted to get it on with her in an alley.

A few insults followed as the man stared at her in horror while he remained lying on the ground and his hand covered where her heeled feet were likely to land again, if she decided otherwise.

PJ leaned forward and the man cowered.

Good for him, PJ thought before taking the jacket he had flung on the rail in the heat of the moment. That was before her senses came back and she realized that she was repeating the same mistake over and over again, by letting a man treat her like a floozy.

She was tired of it all. It was time she took charge of her life and this handsome man who thought she was demented could go to hell as far as she was concerned.

"I think I deserve this," she hissed, holding up the jacket before she turned to hail a cab.

Chad was too stunned to stop her as PJ the demented woman, got into the cab. Sweet mother Mary, he would never have believed that such women existed.

He knew he could have defended himself and not cowered and let her treat him horribly, but his protective male instincts fostered by his forefathers had come to the forefront.

No man was ever allowed to lay a finger on a woman.

Chad groaned in pain from his tender nuts and stood up, glad at the fact that the mad woman was gone. Hopefully he would never ever encounter her. He groaned again as he took a step to the parking lot where he had left his car, not in the mood at all to call his cousin and ask for assistance. The cousin who managed to trick him into all this drama!

He swore under his breath when he got to his car and was reaching forth to the pocket of his non-existent jacket. Luckily PJ had left his pants on, but his keys, phone and wallet were gone.

His house was just a few blocks away, hence he decided to walk. Better yet, he could take in the sights of the nightlife of New York whilst at it.

The more steps he took towards his house, he found himself laughing at the thought of the mad woman. He had been pissed at first by her reaction but now as he thought about it, he saw the hilarity in it.

"You should go out a little more Chad and forget what's her name?" his cousin brother had advised at his house a few hours ago before his life became such a sorry mess.

His young sister and brother-in-law appeared to agree on that. He should have read the signs then that his day had been doomed from the start, especially when his young sister was agreeing to what his crazy cousin was suggesting.

"There are a lot of fish in the pond, waiting to be plucked out," Jeremy had added while Chad looked at his womanizing cousin in horror.

"Please man, don't let us down and be taken down by a mere slip of a woman."

Well, that mere slip of a woman happened to have been his love. They had dated for almost a year and he had popped the question a week ago, thinking she wanted the same thing like him, except Cherise had other ideas.

A week ago, Cherise had looked around the well decorated room that had been made for just that occasion, glanced at his family and friends who were eagerly waiting to hear her reply, just as he was, looked deeply into his eyes before she whispered in regret, "I am sorry Chad but I can't marry you."

His jaw dropped since he wasn't expecting that reply while his eyes almost popped out of their sockets.

"Ok, ok the party is over," his young bulldozer of a sister hollered before she ushered everyone out. Chad was still stunned, frozen on the spot while trying to process what had just happened.

"I thought we had it good," he whined like a woman, hating it the more as he rose from his kneeling position. "We have been dating for a year now and marriage is the next best thing to all this."

"Listen," Cherise held his hands and smiled. "You are a good guy Chad and I love you but..." she chewed at her bottom lip. Nothing good was about to come out, Chad just knew it because every time when a woman said they loved you with a but slotted in, it actually meant the worst was yet to come.

"But I don't think you are ready for such a commitment."

Huh, could the woman hear herself? There he had been, holding out an engagement ring to her and she thought he wasn't ready.

"I mean your finances are not yet set, baby. You still live with your sister and brother-in-law and to top it all off, I will have to travel to the back of beyond and maybe live there too."

"What is wrong with that," he frowned.

"Well Chad this is home to me, I can't go and live in Africa away from civilization."

Good grief, did Cherise just diss his nationality then. She had always known from the moment they met that one day he would have to go back to his home.

The American dream my foot, this was all a fluke, he thought as he saw his girlfriend for the first time on what she really was.

She must have enjoyed parading him around as her 'African boyfriend'. Suddenly it all seemed to make sense, on how she would proudly introduce him to her friends and remark, "Chad is from Safe Haven." Then they would nod pretending to know before she added, "Africa."

He should have realized then why she was always proud to parade him around, except he was madly in love with her and brushed it aside. Now come to think of it Cherise was such a snob.

Cherise smiled at his sister who had been unashamedly listening in on their conversation, wearing a broad smile on her face which was evident for all to see on how she had never liked her brother's girlfriend while Chad's heart broke into a million pieces. She smiled with that apologetic slant of her mouth before she nodded and left.

That young sister who had a wolfish grin on her face was the very same a week later suggesting that he moved on, more vocal in encouraging him to go out and sow his wild oats. She totally understood and would not tell their dear old dad what he was up to in a foreign land.

So, with their ill spoken advice on a Friday night, he finally went out.

As usual his cousin walked into the bar, forty-five minutes later and found him nursing a drink. He was dressed in a brown fur coat and gold necklaces on his neck.

"You know what you look like," he asked Jeremy with a furrowed brow, staring at the pimp known as his cousin brother and got his answer from the grin Jeremy produced that revealed his gold teeth.

"Well, cuz, unlike you I have to use my pocket and not looks to get the girl."

Chad rolled his eyes, using the pocket and looking like a pimp were two different things, he thought and watched Jeremy at work, smiling at the ladies as those who loved bling walked towards him.

Jeremy was more than willing to splurge his money on them.

Handsome pocket, Jeremy mouthed, winked before he walked out of sight with two scantily dressed girls almost half his age. Chad could as well imagine his uncle turning in his grave at what had become of Jeremy in America.

• • ❧ • •

"UNBREAK MY HEEEAAAART; say you will loooove me again. Undo this huuurt you caused when you walked out of the door," PJ sang as tears slid down her beautiful face. Her voice cracked at the last note and her friend Barb was heard hollering, "That's it, you need to get out and stop moping around about that loser Tony."

"Don't you dare call him a loser," she defended.

"Then what is he?"

"He is innocent in all this, Shaz is at fault. She seduced him."

"Can you even hear yourself?" Barb scoffed. "Shaz seduced him just like the other women did right. Poor Tony he is always forced to be in the company of light skirts," she snorted in disgust before she pushed PJ towards the bathroom to get ready for their night out of carousing, as single, young available women.

"I give up on love," PJ said when she came out of the bathroom and let her friend select a dress for her. What she longed for the most was to curl up in bed and weep further for her lost love, but Barb was having none of it. She settled for indifference instead and let Barb take the lead in this, no matter how outrageous what Barb might suggest sounded.

"Twelve years later and you still act in the same way you did when you first came to the city," Barb looked at her with a frown before she threw a black dress at her.

"Wear that," she advised. PJ took the dress and wore it. She pulled at it and asked, "Where is the other half?"

Her friend giggled. "Remember, you promised to let me take the lead in this an hour ago, before you went down the pity party lane and started singing to Toni Braxton."

"I might have, but I didn't mean that you should turn me into a hooker."

"There is a difference between a slutty look and a sexy one. I get why Tony was snagged by Shaz; you have let yourself go."

PJ glared at her friend. Barb pretended not to have noticed the glare but rather busied herself by wearing a red dress that showed off her curvy figure before she settled down on the bed and started applying her makeup.

"Once we are out there in the club, hook up with a handsome guy; make sure he is loaded too."

PJ snorted, "Geez Barb, I wonder how that could be accomplished, should I ask for his bank details the moment he says hi."

Barb rolled her eyes, "I am serious, handsome and loaded is what you need," she advised, rolled back her lipstick then turned to face her. "Why cry in a poky little flat like ours after being ditched by a man. Imagine if you got involved with a rich guy, when he ditched you at least you would be left weeping in a mansion than be back here stuck with your former roommate again."

"There is nothing wrong with this place and neither is Tony's place or his finances."

"There definitely is, for starters Tony doesn't deserve you and you worsened your plight by moving in with him. He had it pretty good since his money was his while you paid for everything."

With the way Barb was laying it out thick, PJ felt like a doormat.

"If I were you girlfriend, I would be painting the town red and saying good riddance to bad rubbish," she finished and resumed with the last touches of her make up before she stood up.

PJ huffed; it was so like Barb to turn her relationship with Tony into nothing but a pile of ash.

"Ok, ok, you know what, I get it. Let's just go and party," PJ ground out before she literally fled from her ever honest friend.

Chapter 2

THEY managed to get into the latest trending club and PJ was shocked at the spectacle that Barb made of herself, twerking like no man's business.

"PJ, I didn't expect to see you here," a voice that she knew so well spoke from behind her. She had left Barb dancing with a guy she came across on the dance floor and was now waiting for her drink. She was feeling parched from all the dancing she had done so she could forget about you know who.

Whirling around, as she had suspected Tony was standing right behind her with his hands in his pockets. She nearly drooled. He looked so handsome. Why is it that she had a weakness for the tall, broody types that spelt trouble?

Not forgetting who had the audacity to cheat on her whilst she was mourning her mom's death.

She sighed and was brought to mother earth when Shaz, her number one enemy at the moment wrapped her claws around Tony.

He turned around and gave her a kiss. After the long kiss, Shaz acted surprised like she was now noticing that PJ was there.

"Aw, hi PJ fancy seeing you here."

The nerve of the woman, pretending like she hadn't noticed me standing near Tony. PJ smiled at the same time wishing she could murder someone.

"Be a darling and order a drink for me honey," Shaz said to Tony before she turned to PJ.

Tony smiled and left the two ladies alone.

He has turned into a puppy that could be told to 'fetch' by dear old Shaz and do just that, PJ thought.

"So how have you been?"

A glass of her favorite martini was slid on the counter towards where she stood. PJ reached out to it and gulped it down quickly before she brightly answered, "Just great," and flicked her finger to the beat.

She wasn't in the mood to make small talk with her former friend. The bartender slid another one and mouthed 'on the house' before he turned to serve other customers. PJ gratefully took the glass and quickly gulped down the contents while Shaz disapprovingly stared at her.

When she was done downing out the contents of her drink, she slid the glass back to the bartender who winked at her before she turned and started walking away.

She hollered, "It has been nice seeing you again Shaz, I see Barb calling out to me on the dance floor."

"PJ wait," her former friend said and touched the sleeve of her dress. PJ looked at her hand and Shaz pulled it back after seeing the glare.

"I am sorry about what happened. Tony loves me and I love him," Shaz said.

"What do you need me for then if you are so in love with each other, hmm?" she furiously asked.

Shaz wrapped her arms around herself in a protective manner before she answered, "We never intended to hurt you. We resisted the growing attraction for a while but it was futile. I was hoping PJ that in due time, you will find it in your heart to forgive us and once we move past the hurdle, we can be friends again."

PJ was lost for words. Was Shaz really serious about this? What sort of sick joke was this? Her becoming friends again with the woman who had betrayed her and taken her man, the girl had some nerve.

She clapped her hands instead; the martini had loosened her up a bit. "Bravo to you. That was a nice speech there and for a second I nearly believed it to be coming from the bottom of your heart." She tilted her head and stared at Shaz arms over her breasts. "Wow, except you don't have one. Kudos to you, you deserve an award for this," as she spoke, her voice raised a notch higher.

"PJ you're causing a scene," Shaz said while her eyes ran around the club.

"Why wouldn't I cause a scene, tell me and don't you dare touch me with those filthy hands of yours," she warned before walking a step further towards the dance floor.

"Listen everybody, this floozy right here," she shouted and pointed at her former friend. "Stole my man and she has the audacity to want to still be friends with me huh!" she chuckled in disbelief. She could feel a few glances glued on her from the spectacle she was making of herself, but she was beyond caring.

"PJ!" Shaz managed to say and looked at her resolutely. PJ knew that look ever since they were kids in that Shaz would have made up her mind on something. Shaz shook her head then trudged on with what she wanted to say, "You will understand once you meet the one."

"And you think Tony wasn't the one for me."

Shaz nodded.

"What makes you think that," PJ yelled. She was already panting with her hand curled in a fist, resisting the urge to slap her former friend.

"Five times, that's how many times Tony has left and come back to me. And you think you are the one for him, stop kidding yourself Shaz," PJ angrily said.

"This time it's different."

PJ looked at her in disbelief.

"We are engaged PJ," Shaz muttered under her breath.

PJ could feel her heart shutter into a million pieces in that instant. Four years and that was the payment she got from being the loyal girlfriend to Tony.

She had stayed with him, cooked and tended to his every need and now he was engaged to her best friend.

She looked at her former friend who was staring at her with pity evident in her eyes and she hated Shaz the more. She hated the fact that Shaz had succeeded where she had failed, to make Tony commit to their relationship.

PJ had tried everything to no avail until finally she resigned herself to being just the girlfriend. She should have listened to her mom who had always advised her never to give it out easily. If a man had the cow at hand and was milking it, what was the use of buying it?

How she suddenly missed her mom.

She continued staring at Shaz. They had been friends ever since they were kids and a man had managed to tear that friendship apart. Shaz smiled at her horrified expression and to PJ it was another stab to her. She was rather enjoying this after all like Barb had insinuated before.

That's it; PJ thought and furiously lunged at Shaz. She was tired of being the civil one in all this and acting all mature while Tony and Shaz had fun even after breaking her heart. Enough was enough.

"PJ," a voice drifted from further away, bringing her back to the present. Everything was the same. People dancing and shouting, Tony walking away to get a drink for his lady and PJ not at all the lunatic she had felt she was.

She gulped down, shocked at having such a vivid imagination, but this PJ did not fight over a man, she was civilized. Her mother's genes were at the forefront when it came to matters of the heart.

Shaz turned to face her after noticing that Tony was further away and wouldn't hear what she had to say.

"You're looking good PJ," she commented and flicked her hair with her finger. The glint of the ring on the finger could not be mistaken. "So do you," PJ swallowed hard, suppressing the emotions before she excused herself and walked away. Her daydream hadn't been far-fetched after all.

Barb must have seen her walking away because PJ could hear her voice shouting her name before she rushed to where she was.

"What's wrong, you look like your aunt has just died?"

PJ rolled her eyes, "I just need to get a bit of fresh air."

"Are you sure, I saw you talking to Shaz a while back?"

"Shaz is engaged to Tony."

"The bitch is whaa," Barb furiously asked, then started removing her earrings. That made PJ chuckle.

"Let her be."

She knew that Barb was capable of acting out her day dream but rather felt it wasn't worth it.

"Are you going to be fine though, I can still go and slap her around a bit you know?"

"I will be fine, just go on and enjoy the dance with that handsome guy looking your way. You will find me home."

"Let's leave together since we came here together in the first place."

PJ shook her head. "It's ok Barb, you don't have to do that. I am fine, I promise. Just continue with what you were doing. You will find me home."

"Alright, don't twist my hand further or my bones will pop out," Barb joked while PJ chuckled. Barb smiled and nodded in understanding to PJ's relief since she desperately wanted to be alone in her misery. Barb hugged her before she turned and walked towards the man she had been dancing with.

PJ sighed and walked out of the club. Once outside, she breathed in the cool fresh air and welcomed its calming effect.

"Hey lady, can you please stand on the side," the security man at the door spoke and PJ huffed. Couldn't people just let her suffer without being a pain to her too? She shifted away from the entrance and walked a few feet to some ladies who were standing on the side. She shivered at the coolness of the weather and tugged at the dress that showed more of her thighs than she would ordinarily reveal.

The weather elements appeared to not be on her side because a slight breeze passed, fluttering her dress and making her shiver while she tugged at the dress again.

A warm coat was draped around her to her shock, which had her looking up to see who her prince charming was.

"Cold," he asked casually like he knew her.

She nodded and muttered, "Thanks."

"Wanna take a walk."

PJ looked at the handsome tall broad-shouldered man standing right in front of her and hesitated for a second before she made up her mind and nodded her head. It wasn't like she had a man waiting for her at home, just that cold bed to go to. The man smiled and motioned with his hand for her to take the lead.

Chapter 3

CHAD couldn't believe his luck. He had all but been thinking that this night was a fluke when he came out of the club ready to call it a night. Jeremy had vanished for the second time with another set of ladies after having advised him, "Sow your wild oats cuz. You are young and you need to live a little."

Chad had gulped down his drink instead and walked out. His heart was just not ready even for him to engage in a little fling.

He had been debating over going to the parking lot or walking home when he caught sight of a beautiful woman tugging at her short dress. She was standing with the rest of the ladies of the night at the side of the club but looked out of place. First timer, he guessed and noticed her shiver.

Why would such a girl choose this kind of profession, he wondered but his mind had already been made. Sex with no strings attached might be what he needed. Better yet, the lady would not even remember him afterwards.

He wouldn't have contemplated this, but she might just be the diversion he needed after all. Three ladies smiled at him. He ignored them, but swiftly walked to the one oblivious of his presence. Noticing another shiver, he took off his jacket and draped it over her shoulders. When she looked up, his breath hitched, she was breathtaking.

"Cold?" he asked in his casual manner, with the hope that she would not flee. She nodded and smiled, taking his breath away before muttering, "Thanks."

"Wanna take a walk?" Chad asked. He could literally see her contemplate before she nodded and he motioned for her to lead. They fell in step with each other.

"I am Chadwick Johnson by the way," he introduced.

"Peggy James, my friends call me PJ."

"Nice to meet you PJ, so what brings you to this wild part of the city?" Chad asked and hoped he hadn't botched up the whole thing. He didn't know how he was meant to talk to a hooker. Did they sit down and chat about their medical history first or did they just get it on. The next time he saw his cousin, he would surely strangle him for suggesting that he have a one-night stand and not be there to guide him.

PJ chuckled instead, not realizing his trepidation. He loved the sound of her laugh, he thought and she looked more beautiful when she smiled.

"My prince charming turned out to be a frog, so here I am, searching for another prince to mend my broken heart."

Chad guessed that was the line she mostly used on her clients. He humored her by standing still and reaching out to her. She stood still. He used his finger to tilt her head by the chin before huskily remarking, "A beautiful princess like you will never fall in short supply of princes and knights. I am yours sweet princess, bewitched by your mesmerizing eyes."

PJ shyly lowered her eyes from the intensity in his, before Chad leaned in for the kiss.

It was hesitant at first as they grew accustomed to each other before it deepened. It was sweet and tender, at the same time a wonder as both were on the quest of discovering that one could feel so strongly about the other in an instant. They slightly drew apart, shocked before they resumed kissing.

PJ squealed in delight when Chad pressed her to the wall. The brother smelled so good and tasted sweeter than honey. He was such a good kisser, she thought as she wrapped her arms around his neck. He ardently kissed her, whispering sweet nothings while he did it in his husky voice. She could taste the bourbon as their tongues stroked and a shiver passed down her spine. He flipped the jacket draped around her and placed it on the rail before he resumed with his ministration and his hand stroked her bare back.

PJ sighed at it all and was engulfed in a warm embrace as her hands also worked on unbuttoning his shirt. She was pressed firmly against his body and could feel every part of him as the kiss went on. The heat emanating from his body, his firm thighs, hard broad chest and the large hands cradling her behind, holding her up so she wouldn't fall.

She was suddenly brought to earth when she caught on what he was saying.

She thought she hadn't heard him correctly and continued kissing him, not wanting to break contact again as his hard body pressed her to the wall. What she needed was comfort and to be made to feel special for one night, if that's what it took to get over Tony's betrayal, except Chad asked, "Is a thousand enough" and drew away from her before innocently looking at her.

No he didn't, PJ thought before it dawned on what he had been thinking, not at all the fairy tale picture she had foolishly painted in her mind.

Could this day get any worse from what it was? First, she was betrayed, and then she found out that her boyfriend was engaged to her best friend and now this handsome hunk, staring at her with tender eyes, thought she was a hooker. Wait until Barb heard about this, it was totally her fault with her silly scrap of clothing she had dressed her in.

"What makes you think I am a lady of the night?" she asked softly and shifted from his arms. Chad looked at her in horror and she could see the uncertainty cloud his face. "Well, are you not, you were standing with the rest of the girls and I assumed you were since you quickly accepted my offer for the walk."

Well lucky me, when did accepting a walk spell hooker, PJ almost yelled but stopped herself from ranting at him. She thought hard and nodded. "Ok, if you increase to two k, I will be yours for the sampling," she said, pulling on her most seductive smile and damning the man to hell.

What had she been thinking?

Her prince had suddenly turned into a man with a fetish for the girls of the night. She watched him smile before he opened his arms to her.

Chad had been horrified that he had made another blunder, but was relieved when PJ smiled and moved into his arms. One moment he was kissing her and the next writhing in pain on the ground while she hailed some insults at him.

The charming lady had turned into a crazy demented one. The rest was history.

He should never have listened to Jeremy and Meghan, Chad thought while he walked to the house which he shared with his young sister and her family. Once he reached home, he rapped on the door in the hopes that Meghan would hear it.

He wasn't ready to ring the bell and wake everyone up. Everyone happened to be nosey and right now all he wanted was a good night's sleep and not an interrogation.

"What happened to you," his sister groggily asked when she answered the door. Of course, his ever-perceptive sister would notice the fact that he didn't have his favorite jacket with him. He settled for an angrily said, *mugged bit,* hoping she would not enquire much. He glared at her to stop her from asking further before he walked towards his room. He could hear her chuckle. Of course, she didn't believe him because he was a great fighter after all and in no way would he ever be mugged in his life.

Plopping on the bed like dead weight, he drifted off to sleep, only to be ranted on by that demented woman in his sleep again.

Chapter 4

CHAD didn't sleep for long because the next moment he was being woken up by his nephew of twelve years.

"You're going to thank me for this," his nephew excitedly said while Chad looked at his clock and groaned before chucking out his bed sheet and getting up.

"Thank you for what?" he asked but their conversation was interrupted by his sister shouting for the young Watson to get ready for school.

Nick dashed from the room before Chad could ask further. Walking to his private bathroom, he got ready for work.

"Morning" his sister greeted once he was done and he got into the kitchen.

"Morning uncle," his cute niece greeted and held out her arms. Chad loved his princess to bits. He gladly picked her up and made some smacking kissing sounds on her cute chubby cheeks while she giggled.

"Are you ready partner?" Robin, his brother-in-law, asked while getting into the room. Chad smiled at him and placed Melisa back on the ground. He patted his jacket, "Where are my damn keys."

That had Meghan laughing.

"You really must have been out of it for you to forget this quickly."

He swore when the image of a passionate, demented woman filtered into his mind.

"Hey mind your language, they are kids here."

"Sorry sis."

"No need to worry uncle, I have it all handled, Nicholas to the rescue. The perv has been caught. She is in jail," his nephew said simply to Chad's horror.

"What do you mean the perv has been caught," he asked, dreading what his twelve-year-old nephew had been up to while he slept. Nick loved playing cop and robbers ever since he was a toddler and this was getting out of hand.

"Mom mentioned that you had been mugged, so I tracked your phone and called it in."

Damn and another damn to boot. Chad groaned. Why did he have to get a computer geek for a nephew, from what he had witnessed about PJ, he doubted she could take whatever had been done to her lightly.

"Robin, we should leave before I kill your son and wife."

"Why would you kill me?" Meghan asked innocently.

"Well, you told your son I had been mugged."

Robin raised his hand in surrender before sister and brother got into their native shouting match as they usually did. He motioned for his son to leave and trailed behind him. Chad must have noticed that they had vacated the room because he soon followed after.

It was after they had dropped his son off at his school while going to the station that Robin stopped the car and turned to Chad.

"What is going on Chad, didn't your boy's night out go well and were you not mugged like you mentioned to Meghan."

Chad rolled his eyes and narrated the events that took place while Robin roared in laughter. "I can't wait to see this ..." Robin cleared his throat before finishing, "hooker. She definitely is one of a kind."

"It was a reasonable mistake; let's just say my senses had been dulled by the alcohol I consumed."

Chad sat back on the seat before motioning for Robin to drive, "Enough about this, just drive will you."

"Hooker," Robin shook his head rather enjoying it. "How could you assume such a thing? Hookers are not classy like you described her and they definitely don't wear expensive perfume."

"How would you know, have you cheated on my sis with a hooker before?"

"You know damn well that I would never do such. She's the love of my life, if I hurt her, I lose everything."

Chad nodded. He knew what his young sister and Robin had gone through in order to finally be together. They had proved their love not only to each other but to those close to them. Interracial marriages might have been common in America, but they weren't that common in their Island.

"Just drive man," Chad commanded.

"Aye, aye captain," his brother-in-law said with a laugh. Chad already regretted telling him the whole thing. Robin would tell his wife and only the Lord knew what his nosy sister would do with the information. He groaned and touched his forehead, dreading what awaited him at his workstation.

· · ❧ · ·

"I'M GOING TO BREAK his neck when I see him, shred his heart to strips and toss his body in a garbage can," PJ said while the two officers laughed and one hollered, "Serial killer on the loose, we sure are glad to have caught you before you caused any more damage."

After dropping off a few blocks from her apartment, PJ got into yet another bar where she drank herself to oblivion. She wanted to numb it all out. She didn't want to feel the pain anymore, the rejection and betrayal. Where was Barb when she needed her?

Perry the bartender had woken her up and insisted on taking her home, except she grabbed his keys and he was forced to clutch at the side of the seat while she had her reckless joy ride and a police van stopped them right on time.

Now in the cell she whimpered softly and finished the remainder of her bottle of wine.

"You know officer, you are a good man," she said to the friendly officer who had been kind enough to listen to her sob story while his partner scoffed and remarked, "Daniels, this is all on you, when the captain comes in and questions why we have a cell with booze in it, please kindly explain that I am not involved."

PJ darted her tongue out and rolled her eyes at the stern officer, serves him right. His eye was slowly becoming purple. She giggled and pointed at it. He huffed and threw up his hands in the air, before he walked away.

A lady officer leaned in with a cup of coffee that she handed to Officer Daniels.

He took it and walked to PJ. "Drink this," he advised.

"Why should I?" she sulked instead. Daniels shrugged his shoulders and placed the cup next to her, before he picked the bottle up and turned to leave.

"What is going on here Daniels," his captain asked and his knees nearly buckled. To worsen matters, PJ giggled, stumbled to where he stood and said, "Who has graced us with their presence in our humble abode." To his horror, she wrapped her arms around him while he tried to get away from the fumes of alcohol in her breath. Obrien, the lady officer who had made the coffee, had scrambled off the moment she spotted the captain.

So much for trying to help out the poor girl, he was now in hot soup.

"Captain, it's not what you are thinking."

Chad crossed his arms over his chest and narrowed his eyes. "And what is it that I am thinking?"

Officer Marks came back and smirked at Daniels with an, I told you so expression while Daniels looked for a way to get out of this hitch.

"She was arrested for over speeding, driving under the influence, trying to bribe an officer of the law, when she didn't succeed, assault as you can see my eye, kidnapping of a petrified barman," officer Marks gladly recited and continued to add more of her crimes.

"I believe this belongs to you captain; it was in her possession when we caught her." Chad looked at the jacket and his eyes widened before he looked back for the second time at the girl.

That beautiful girl who had kicked him in the nuts for being mistaken for a hooker was standing right in front of him with her arms still clinging to Daniels. Her hair was disheveled and her eyes puffy. He looked at what Daniels was holding as his Officer tried to hide it behind his back.

He slowly and surely was getting furious. And to think he had almost killed his sister and nephew over meddling. It was turning out to be a good thing that his nephew had reported his missing jacket as he could evidently see that PJ at the moment was not fit to be in good society.

Daniels reached out to the coffee and advised PJ, "Please drink this."

PJ refused and pouted her lips. Officer Marks reached for the coffee instead and muttered, "No use throwing away good coffee."

Chad almost flagged his hands at his incompetent officers. The one day he decided to take himself out and already he found such a disaster.

"You," PJ spoke up when she recognized him. She glared at him. "This is the man with the fetish who mistook me for a hooker."

Officer Marks was in the process of drinking the coffee when PJ said that, spat out his coffee before he stifled the urge to laugh.

The captain glowered at him. That had him straightening to his full stature, coughing before he excused himself, leaving his partner to stew in his own mess.

"Did you contact any of her family members or friends," Chad asked Daniels who nodded in reply. "Take her out of the cell," he advised.

"Captain are you sure," Daniels asked while Chad glared at him. "You've already done more damage, do what I say."

Daniels opened the door to the cell and assisted PJ to walk out of it while an unsuspecting Captain was shocked when she suddenly hurled herself at him and ran her hands over his face remarking, "You look even more handsome today."

Daniels smothered his laughter and mumbled, "I tried to warn you."

Chapter 5

"WHERE is that crazy lil sis of mine," Barb asked when she got into the captain's office after getting the reply to enter. She already had a story made up to explain PJ's bender. She shouldn't have listened to her the night before when she bravely said she was okay and would leave for home. Her well made-up story died down the moment she came face to face with the captain.

"Chad."

"Barb." He said and grinned at her.

"I see you still have a knack for attracting the wrong friends."

Barb flagged her arms dismissively and walked towards him. "Just give me a hug and forget about my friends for a bit, it's been a long time."

Chad laughed. Barb hadn't changed at all. He hugged her and she pulled back before clutching his arms and remarking, "You have gotten stronger and sexier."

"And you dated my cousin."

She huffed while his grin widened. Barbara learnt with his little sis that's how they knew each other too before the whole Jeremy thing. She and Jeremy dated for a mere month until she caught him cheating and left. Till to date his womanizing cousin cried whenever he thought about her.

"Yaa, we get it Barb, he is your former lover and still looks great with his abs intact," PJ mumbled, bringing them to the awareness of another occupant in the room.

"PJ," Barb shrieked and glared at her friend who couldn't see her outraged expression due to having a cold damp towel over her face.

She snorted and turned to face Chad, "Don't mind my mad friend Chad; she lost her mom a month ago and caught her boyfriend cheating when she came back from the burial that is why she is being a b..."

Chad nodded in sympathy and sat back on the chair.

"So, when did you get transferred to this precinct?"

"I have been here for three months now," he replied. They continued to chat for a while before Chad went back to the woman who was lazily lying on his couch in the office and passing silly comments at whatever they said.

Barb looked horrified at hearing about what her best friend had been up to. "I am sure she can't be the same sweet Pea that I know," Barb said. Chad resisted the urge to roll his eyes. Everyone was acting crazy around him, from his officer Daniels who had plied more booze to PJ, Marks who wanted justice for the blackened eye and now to her best friend who claimed she wasn't in any way the woman he was seeing.

He ran his eyes over her sexy long legs and wished he had a fleece to cover those sexy thighs. The dress was too revealing, especially in broad daylight.

The jacket would be too obvious and knowing Barb, she would marry them off in an instant if she realized he was attracted to her not so sober friend.

"PJ is kind, sweet, and considerate, not at all the lunatic you met yesterday, I promise."

An image of the sweet girl he had approached flicked in his mind until he ruined it and got the demented woman after mistaking her for a hooker. He cringed at the thought. Robin was right, how could he liken the lady with the silken thighs to a hooker.

She shifted and he gulped down a few breaths before scratching at his chin.

He was partly to blame. His instincts had been dulled to notice the vulnerability in her eyes when she mentioned the prince who left her.

She had been hurting and he added more to her injury by thinking of getting a diversion from her.

"Is she going to be ok," he finally asked and looked pointedly at PJ. After he got her out of the cell, he had taken her to his office and given her more and more coffee to bring her to her senses. Why he even felt concerned, he wondered.

"She will be fine," Barb answered. "I fear for her sanity though. Once she returns to normal, she will avoid everyone like a plague."

Chad chuckled while Barb sighed.

"If only you had met her that night when I set you both up for a blind date, maybe this wouldn't have happened at all."

"I can hear you, Barb by the way. Stop throwing me at every male person in your vicinity. With Chad I can give an exception if he apologized for calling me a hooker."

Barb turned to him and crossed her arms over her breasts, glaring at him with accusation in her eyes. "The plot thickens," Barb commented.

"That was a mistake," he said mildly.

She went back to talking to him, ignoring her friend, "By the way, I heard about your breakup with Cherise." Chad's mouth thinned as he imagined strangling his young sis for being a blabbermouth. Did she call the whole freaking town and tell them how he was dumped? They were only a few close friends and relations when it happened.

"Her loss PJs gain," Barb added.

"You really are selling your friend; I get why she is complaining in her intoxicated state and failing to sleep. Who knows she might wake up in a strange house?" Chad commented.

"I am serious," Barb said. "You and PJ would be perfect for each other. You have no social lives, are workaholics and picky when it comes to people you associate with."

"Thank you Barb for making me sound boring," PJ and Chad both said in unison. One was glaring while the other one's voice was muffled by the towel still on her face.

Barb laughed. "You see. Common ground, that's progress. Anyways I should get going; it's time I took my best friend home."

Chad stood up from behind his desk. When Barb reached the couch, she stood with her arms akimbo for a while before she took the towel off PJ's face. "Explain yourself, young lady," she said while PJ cringed from the splitting headache that was beginning to set in. She was sleep deprived and her world was still spinning despite the handsome captain having plied her with a larger amount of bitter coffee than she has ever consumed in a lifetime.

"Let's just go home," she mumbled before she stood up. She swayed and Chad caught her before she could fall and continued to sweep her off her feet. If she hadn't been feeling that terrible from the splitting headache, she could have thought the action romantic and enjoyed being in his arms more.

"I will have you know that I am capable of walking on my own," she mumbled and wound her arms around his neck before laying her head and shutting her eyes. Chad scoffed while Barb giggled on the side.

"Barb, are you sure this is the self-assured divorce lawyer you wanted me to meet for a blind date."

"Guys I can hear you; you know that right."

"Be grateful everyone dropped the charges," Barb said. Barb walked ahead and opened the door for Chad who assisted PJ get in the backseat.

"You take care of yourself, love and thank you for everything," Barb said before she hugged Chad and drove out of the parking lot.

"That handsome captain called me a hooker and still he didn't apologize for it," PJ sniffled while Barb retorted, "You hit him in the nuts and assaulted another police officer after him."

Tears ran down PJs face and Barb could hear her sniffle. She cursed Tony in her heart for making her friend so miserable. "Honey, I do pray when you are sober enough and remember this, you will not hide for a month from everyone in your room," she commented as she drove PJ home.

Chapter 6

PJ was coming from the ladies when she heard the deep familiar voice she had come to associate with the handsome captain.

It was a month after her little episode. Like what her friend had said, she was avoiding everyone like a plague, especially Chad.

He was the first in line. Salma the waitress flagged her hands to her while PJ tried to stop her from doing so, indicating with her hands too.

"PJ," Salma called as she quickly made a retreat out of the café.

Salma shrugged her shoulders, "Guess she was in a hurry," she commented to Chad who smiled and got his order.

"Let me get that too," Chad settled the bill and got PJ's order before he walked out of the restaurant. It was time to say 'hello' to the crazy woman who was always ducking and escaping when she caught sight of him.

He saw her walking at a fast trot and pulled over.

"Want a lift," he asked.

PJ was startled from her thoughts and shut her eyes briefly, wishing for the ground to open up and swallow her. That dreaded meeting was happening earlier than anticipated. Peeking through the open window, she put on her most charming smile.

"Hi Chad. Thanks for the offer but I'm good and the building is just up ahead."

"Just get in PJ, I will not bite," he opened the door for her. A blast of a hooter sounded from behind, which had her quickly scrambling into the car since she wasn't ready to receive some insults from angry motorists too.

Chad drove the car in silence while she fidgeted on her seat.

She sat up straight. She could do this. Turning to face him she cleared her throat and said, "I am sorry."

Chad drove to the side before he stopped the car and turned to her. Now she was going to hear the reprimand. Apparently, his co-workers respected him and he was good at what he did. Of course, she found out that fact from Barb and Daniels who she had gone out to dinner with a couple of times afterwards.

"Why are you apologizing, I should be the one doing so."

PJ's mouth fell open before she snapped it shut, not having expected that.

"W—h—y..." she stuttered, "Why would you apologize to me?"

"Well because I failed to notice how vulnerable you were that night and only had one thought in mind, to get you naked."

PJ coughed and wheezed while Chad patted her back. This was going to be harder than she thought. Returning to the topic at hand, she asked, "How would you have known, we were complete strangers then?"

Chad shrugged his shoulders and sat back on the seat. He heaved a sigh before he asked, "Can we start over."

PJ was relieved too, especially when he smiled at her and she felt her tummy flutter. She could definitely do with a new slate.

"I am Chadwick Johnson and I don't think you are a hooker," he said.

"Peggy James and I also don't think you are a pervert," she giggled and stretched out her hand. She looked in wonder as Chad caught her hand with both his large ones before she felt his warm lips on her hand and inhaled sharply.

The sexual chemistry wasn't alcohol induced like she had thought before, seeing she was as sober as a judge now but her body was responding the same way. It was official. She was a hooker.

"Nice to meet you PJ," he said before letting her hand go and pulling back into the road. She clutched on the seatbelt, fearing she might hurl herself at him if she didn't.

"We are here," Chad spoke up. For a second there she had been in a daze. She looked out of the window and noted that she indeed had arrived at the building before she quickly opened the door and scrambled out.

"PJ."

She peeked through the window. He reached at the back for something before he handed it to her. "Your lunch," he explained.

Damn, he saw her skulking off after all. She smiled briefly, said a thank you, before rushing to the building where she worked. Chad chuckled and was driving away when he noticed her purse on the seat. She had been in such a rush that she forgot it.

"Who is the man who drove you back here," Tony asked while PJ rolled her eyes. "It's none of your business, you are not my father." She continued walking, trying to ignore him, but he followed her to her office. "How can I help you Mr. Clark, I believe your office is a floor above."

"You know PJ, I knew that you were cheating on me. Who is this guy who brought you back from your lunch?"

Seriously, she wasn't ready to deal with this crap.

"What happened to your fiancée Shaz? Has the novelty of love at first sight worn off and she discovered what a lousy lay you are?"

"PJ!" he yelled.

"That will take some time before they are done," someone remarked from behind Chad. He turned to face the person. After noticing that PJ had left her purse, he had parked the car at a handicapped spot before he rushed to get to her. He didn't mean to eavesdrop on the conversation going on, but the two parties' muffled voices were certainly getting louder even though he couldn't get what they were saying.

"PJ left her purse in my car," he said as a way of explaining and handed it to the woman. "Please make sure she gets it."

The lady nodded. A crush sounded that had Chad and the lady jumping. "Shouldn't someone go in and stop them?"

The lady giggled. "Don't worry. They do that all the time, break up and make up." Chad nodded and looked to the door where the angry voices were coming from.

"Ok, make sure, she gets that," he said again before he walked out of the place as fast as he could.

"Thelma, Dana, Bridget, Lucy, Mary and now Shaz, who is the cheater here," PJ yelled.

"That is beside the point. Who was that guy?" Tony yelled back.

"You know what; I am not going to have this conversation with you." She sat on her chair and opened her laptop. "You can use the door to see yourself out."

"The reason I wanted to talk to you," Tony ground out, inhaled deeply, pasted his boyish smile and calmly looked at PJ before saying, "I am here to talk about the Gilbert's anniversary."

"What about it?"

"Remember I am garnering to be a partner in the firm..."

Mmmhm that she knew, booty licking the boss so he got that.

Mr. Gilbert was the owner of the law firm and also happened to be her uncle. Recently he had announced his intention of adding another partner into the mix.

Mr. Gilbert and his wife were meant to celebrate their anniversary a week from now. PJ was beginning to think that Tony had only been interested in her because of her uncle, seeing here he was gritting his teeth and throwing his pride away so he asked to attend the party with her. He was such a snake.

"I thought we could go to their anniversary together. Be the power couple that we usually are."

PJ scoffed; she had been right after all with her line of thought. "Doesn't the hairdresser suit your ambitions in that front," she glibly asked.

"As you know Mr. Gilbert likes seeing us together."

PJ sat back on the chair, crossed her legs and her arms. "The old man will have to get over it, because we aren't together anymore. What if I decide to join this rat race and booty licking that is going on so I'm made partner?"

Tony laughed.

"I am serious, I am good at what I do and I have brought in some high-powered cases."

"Divorce cases," Tony ground out before he smiled again and had that glint in his eyes that said I have another stupid idea. "Speaking about divorce, family matters to him. I expect when he sees a ring on that finger of yours all will be forgiven." PJ reached to her picture frame and hurled it at Tony who quickly dodged it as it hit the wall and broke.

She smiled sweetly before she answered, "I can't attend the party as your fiancée because as hard as it might be for you to believe. I have moved on and have a man in my life." She couldn't believe the nerve Tony had, pretending that he wasn't engaged to her former friend and that she would entertain him like before. What had she seen in him anyways, to make her go back to him every time he apologized after messing up?

"Liar," Tony ground out.

"Mind refresher, the guy you were whining about just a minute ago. You saw him and how you pale in comparison with him. He is what you are not."

Tony angrily walked to her chair before bending over and staring into her eyes.

"What are you doing," PJ shifted back to her seat. She inhaled deeply while he bent over and kissed her. She nearly laughed when her body slightly responded and all of a sudden went cold when deep brown eyes filtered in her mind. Slapping Tony hard on the face before wiping off her lips, she triumphantly said, "I guess your little test proves to you that I am way over you. Like I mentioned, my man is the best."

Tony's veins nearly burst on his forehead, his nostrils flared and his hands clenched on the side. He raised his hand as PJ realized she had taken it too far and flinched. A knock on the door, brought them to the present and had Tony whirling around and storming out from the office.

"Hi Jane, what's up," PJ greeted the lady who had been unceremoniously shoved by the door by an angry Tony as he left.

Jane walked in and handed her the purse, "A tall handsome gentleman brought that. He said you forgot it in his car."

Chad. PJ shut her eyes momentarily. "For how long did he stand by the door?"

"Briefly."

PJ nodded. "Please do send someone to clean up the mess on the corner," she advised before she resumed with her work.

Chapter 7

PJ walked up the front porch and drew in a lot of air into her lungs before she exhaled. The house was impressive from the outside, she thought as she tried to steady her pounding heart.

PJ rang the bell and waited. Barb had been over protective when she had pleadingly asked for Chad's number.

Her friend had gone through a million questions before she cautioned, "I hope he is not a rebound and you will not be tucking your tail going to that loser boyfriend after breaking Chad's heart."

Like she would do such a thing to Chad, just like every male, Chad might not have a heart after all.

"Hi," Chad greeted her, before opening the door wider and letting her into the house.

When she finally mustered up the courage to call him after she got the number from Barb, he had informed her that he was home, babysitting his niece and nephew for the night. The anniversary was closely approaching and Tony never ceased to pop his head into her office in order to goad her, while she wished to cut his balls out.

Looking appreciatively around the modernly decorated living room, she commented, "Nice place." The house had a classy feel and at the same time managed to make one feel at home.

Chad opened his mouth to answer when suddenly a little girl of about four rushed to him. PJ stared at him in wonder as he scooped the girl up and kissed her chubby cheeks.

"Uncle is she your girlfriend," she asked sweetly while Chad coughed and cleared his throat.

"Hi there," PJ stretched out her hand. "I am PJ, your uncle's friend."

The girl pasted a gap-toothed adorable smile. "I am Melisa. You're pretty," she giggled and hid her face on her uncle's neck.

"Ooh thank you" PJ said. "Look at me sweetie, don't be shy." Melisa looked up and PJ smiled, "You're pretty, just like a princess."

"I am a princess," Melisa answered and PJ chuckled at her innocence.

"Mommy is the princess of Surface, so that means I am a princess too."

Chad placed his niece on the ground, "That's enough, you can go on and play with your brother," he spoke softly and watched his niece rush back to the playroom.

"Want to join me in the kitchen while I rustle up a meal," Chad asked.

"You cook."

He nodded and PJ followed him to the kitchen, loving his place the more.

"Now Chad is very different, he stays with his young sister and her family. Says it puts some semblance of self-control in his life. So, he will not be having sex with you anytime soon," Barb had said to PJ.

Sex was totally out of the question. She was blind to his tall frame, sexy body encased in those dark jeans and white t-shirt. This was purely business, that's the reason she was in his house in the first place and it totally had nothing to do with the spine-tingling sensations she felt when close to him ever since the first time they met.

The hot passionate kiss she had received from him didn't brand her. Look Tony was able to make her traitorous body respond briefly that is, rather surprising indeed since before she would have landed back in bed with Tony and back in his life, having packed her bags and returned to his apartment.

She should have listened to the pastor who preached that sex made one stupid, maybe she wouldn't be in this dilemma after all and seeking help from Chad to be her pretend boyfriend.

"You can get settled, I will not bite," Chad said with a smile and winked, making her tummy flutter as usual. She giggled and walked further into the kitchen before she settled on the stool and assisted him by chopping the tomatoes.

She forgot the purpose of why she was actually there as she helped Chad prepare the supper and they talked pertaining to everything. She couldn't remember a time she had felt comfortable in the company of a man, and not had to pretend to be something she was not.

The kids came into the dining room once they were done and PJ witnessed at first hand the love that Chad had for his nephew and niece. The children were loud and PJ found Nick to be a delight as he spoke about wanting to be a cop like his dad and uncle.

It was after supper when she was putting the plates on the shelves after drying them that Chad came to retrieve some glasses on the top shelf.

The kitchen suddenly felt tiny as they stood close and stared at each other. PJ inhaled the spicy aftershave he wore and nearly swooned in a pool on the spot. She licked her lips and could swear her breath was coming in small quick gasps. Now was the time to bring out the good book on why such scenarios spelt trouble. She could feel the heat emanating from his body as he stood close and the slight smile told her enough. He was attracted to her as she was to him.

"We want ice cream, we want ice cream," the children chanted, cutting into the sizzling sexual tension that filled the atmosphere and bringing them back to earth. Chad pulled away and cleared his throat. "You don't mind right," he asked, then shifted further, distancing himself from her and sat the glasses on the counter.

"We usually walk to the ice-cream van after supper."

A slight shiver passed down her spine as PJ suddenly felt cold and wrapped her body protectively with her arms. She cleared her throat, nodded and followed, sighing in relief at the fact that she hadn't hurled herself at him.

She had been a few seconds from doing so. For once she wished to drink a bucket full of alcohol and do just that before she blamed it on the alcohol.

The van was a few blocks away. "Want to taste my ice cream," Melisa asked while she sat on PJ's lap.

PJ shook her head. They were sitting on the chairs near the ice cream van. A few people who liked an evening snack were there too with their families and friends.

"Thank you sweetie but I don't eat...." PJ gulped down in shock as the little girl had already spooned the ice cream with nuts into her mouth when she opened it to speak. Reaching out to the napkin on the side, she spit out the nuts while Chad chided his niece for being naughty.

"Are you going to be okay," he asked. She nodded and smiled reassuringly. Chad had instantly taken Melisa away when he noticed PJs horror while Nick curiously stared at her.

"Are you sure?"

PJ didn't think she had consumed a lot of the nuts for them to have an effect, so she nodded her head, besides she didn't want to scare Melisa.

"Finish up your ice creams so that we go back," Chad advised the children. PJ ate her chocolate minted ice cream, relieved that Chad wasn't looking at her strangely anymore like she would pop.

As they walked back to the house, she scratched her neck, her nose was getting stuffy and her ears itched.

"PJ" Chad frowned.

"I am perfectly fine."

He cursed before he motioned for her to sit still outside the pharmacy they were passing through while Melisa took one look and shrieked, "I have turned aunt PJ into a monster."

"Don't cry, it's nothing, I will be fine."

"Nick take care of PJ and your sister," Chad advised the nephew.

"It can't be that bad," she spoke to Nick who laughed before motioning to the mirror near the entrance of the pharmacy.

She stood up, not paying heed to Chad's advice to remain still and entered the shop. One glance had her screaming like a banshee. That only used to happen while she was at elementary before she knew she was allergic to peanuts. Seeing Shrek looking back at her in the mirror, with the handsome captain nearby was a no, no.

"PJ." Chad rushed to her with the over-the-counter antihistamine for her mild reaction. Her face was swollen; her lips big like a bee had kissed her while her eyes had become two tiny slits. Did she even have eyes?

"Where are my eyes," she hysterically spoke while Nick hollered in laughter at his uncle's funny girlfriend.

Chad hugged her and whispered, "Now I have to deal with two hysterical women," when his niece started crying again.

When they reached the house, Nick was ready to dash off from the company of two bawling girls so he could laugh his lungs out, while the uncle tried to calm both at the same time."

Chad handed PJ the medicine and ordered her to go and lie down on the bed in his room while he put his niece to bed.

By the time he was done, the medicine was taking effect and PJ was feeling drowsy.

"How is she?" she asked about his niece.

"She is now sleeping."

PJ shyly covered her face, "I look ugly" she whispered and looked the other way. The bed dipped as Chad sat on it before he lay next to her and turned her over. "I think you are adorable," he said, taking her hands off her face.

She scoffed and inhaled sharply when he leaned in and tenderly kissed her swollen eyes and lips.

"You know Chad, you are a really nice guy," she commented drowsily while she was drawn into his arms. "And you still remain adorable despite your puffy eyes and lips. I just wish I could take a pic of you, post it on my wall to fend off all the men who may..." he never got to finish his statement but winced in pain and nearly cried like a baby. The woman really knew how to knee the right spot.

"Chad are you ok," PJ asked with concern, hoping she hadn't hurt him that much to the point he would need surgery.

"I will survive," he ground out after shifting away from her. "I don't know if my precious cargo is fine though. Stop messing with my descendants' woman."

She giggled and lay back again having sat up when she heard him groan. "If you learn on how to talk to me, your line will remain intact. What was it that you were saying about posting me on your wall?"

"Nothing," he squeaked while PJ giggled. In a normal voice he asked, "Am I allowed to hug you, or I would get another kick for that."

"This once you are allowed to do so, because I am feeling generous and I really really like you." Chad chuckled at the fact that the next morning she might try to avoid him like before. He pulled her into his arms and kissed the top of her head.

"Chad, the reason why I came today is because I want to ask you something."

"What do you want to ask?"

She yawned and snuggled deeply into his arms, their bodies melding together like one.

"Will you marry me?"

"Huh?" Chad was startled by the question that he asked, "What do you mean," except PJ didn't hear him because she had drifted off to sleep.

Chapter 8

PJ snuggled up deeply in the covers before she opened her eyes and found herself in an unfamiliar room. She blinked as everything filtered back into focus. Of course, she was in Chad's bed after all. What, did the guy also have a fetish for cool things seeing his room was perfect with the soft sheets that were rubbing her skin and almost making her moan? She rushed out of bed to his bathroom and sighed in relief before patting her cheeks.

"Welcome back my beautiful face," she said and looked at all sides of it in the mirror. The swelling was gone. She smiled wickedly before she clutched at her body noticing for the first time she only had her black lacy panties on.

Oh hell, she thought at the recollection of feeling hot during the night and kicking a dead weight out of bed. She stared at her reflection in horror. No, she didn't.

Yes, you did, her reflection spoke back to her. *Kicked Chad out of his own bed.* She groaned at the recollection.

"PJ" a slight knock followed with a lady getting into the room. PJ peeped through the door.

"Oh sorry, you are not yet dressed."

Now she was getting more embarrassed.

"I am Meghan, Chad informed me about yesterday's incident. Get ready and come join me for breakfast," the lady continued before she left the room.

What must his sister think of her? She shrugged her shoulders and shut the door to the bathroom before she got into the shower and welcomed the spray of hot water on her skin. She was done with the shower and smearing lotion on her legs when she heard someone moving around in the bedroom.

"PJ, I've left some clean clothes for you to wear, I think we're the same size," Meghan hollered from behind the door.

"Thanks," PJ shouted back and went back to finishing her toiletry. For an ordinary cop, Chad seemed to enjoy the luxuries offered in life. She went into the bedroom and found the outfit Meghan had left for her on the bed.

Sashaying in the blue slacks that perfectly fit her, she took the chiffon blouse and noticed the tag. A strangled sound issued from her throat at the price tag. Clean clothes my foot, these were brand new designer clothes. Great, there was even a bag and matching shoes that turned out to be her perfect fit.

"Are you sure these are your clothes," she asked when she got into the kitchen where Meghan was.

"Pretty old," Meghan answered with a smile and handed her a plate with hot breakfast.

"With the D&G tag on?" She showed her the tag she had removed. "Ooh that." Meghan chewed at the bottom of her lip before she heaved a sigh. "Ok Chad purchased the clothes for you. He gave me the card; it's a way of apologizing for what Mel did to you. He also mentioned that he called your workplace and informed them that you were sick."

PJ nodded. Right, nothing unusual there, except Chad had literally taken control of her life.

"Speaking about your handsome brother, where is he?"

"He's at work," Meghan answered before she joined PJ and settled next to her. PJ moaned at the first bite of her breakfast while Meghan chuckled. "You and your brother surely know how to prepare a mean meal."

"I am surprised Chad showed you that side of him," Meghan replied instead. "And I found you naked in his room too."

PJ gulped down the coffee quickly and screamed, "Hot, hot." Meghan handed her an ice tray she had placed on the table in case she needed to temper her coffee. PJ dabbed the ice cube on her tongue. "I shwear," she rolled her eyes and chewed at the ice cube before swallowing. "I swear it's not what you think. Nothing happened with your brother last night. Your kids are safe, they were not polluted."

Meghan laughed, "You're funny and I like you."

"What do you mean by that side of him; didn't he prepare a meal for his girlfriend?" Meghan shook her head, "The only thing Cherise knew was on how to spend his money and demand more. He was her money pond until he put an end to it."

PJ chuckled and continued to eat. She thought Meghan's face looked familiar but from where did she see her. When she was finishing up on her coffee that's when it dawned, "Class of 2018, you graduated with Barb four years back."

"For a lawyer, you are surely slow," Meghan said with a chuckle. What Melisa had said, drifted back too and had PJ coughing and clutching her throat as it suddenly dawned on who Meghan was. An actual princess living in the neighborhood. She remembered Barb saying it in passing, that meant Chad...ooh my, which also explained the pricey clothes and not forgetting the modern looking house with all its luxurious furniture.

Cherise must have been blind not to notice the pond of gold she was swimming in. PJ gulped down a few breaths and fanned her face. "How is Safe Haven?"

At that Meghan did laugh loudly. "Relax; I haven't grown two horns all of a sudden. At least you still act normal."

"I just didn't expect...."

Meghan nodded in understanding.

"Did Cherise know?"

"Girl, I wouldn't tell the secret to that twit," Meghan said. "Chad just likes keeping that aspect about himself private. He is an ordinary person making a living just like everyone else."

Ya right, one with expensive taste and who would have to return to take his rightful place, PJ thought.

Bummer, double bummer, she thought as her plans went down the drain. She couldn't ask that favor of him after all. Meghan studied her for a bit before she stated, "You can tell me what's bothering you."

PJ resignedly explained her dilemma to her.

"You can still go ahead and ask him. There is nothing wrong with that."

"Then in no time everyone would know and he will be forced to go back to Safe Haven as a matter of urgency."

"No one knew about his relationship with Cherise back home. He was going to break the news after he proposed. So, you asking him to take you on a one-day date is not a matter of national security."

"Right."

Chapter 9

DANIELS whistled at PJ the moment she stepped into the premises and asked to meet Chad. She gulped down a few breaths before she knocked on Chad's door.

She enjoyed chatting with Meghan and reminiscing over home too. Now how was she meant to address Chad, Your highness, Majesty or prince?

How would she have known that the man who kissed her after she confessed about her frog was an actual prince?

"Just be yourself," Meghan had said, "And propose to Chad again," she continued with a giggle. So apparently Chad told his sister how she asked him to marry her in her medicated state. Another blunder in her not so pristine character where he was concerned. She was meant to ask for a date, not drowsily ask for marriage.

She looked heavenwards feeling disappointed in herself for being such a hussy ever since she met him. Maybe these were side effects of being with Tony for too long, and now her hormones had suddenly awakened to what was out there.

The Tony effect was finally over and for good. At some point Tony's cheating and sob stories stopped having the effect they once had on her. For a couple of months, she had battled feeling disgusted and repulsed by even the slight thought of sleeping with him. She had been disquieted about these feelings until she heard some of her clients open up and confide that they had the same feeling and experience too before seeking counsel for divorce.

She opened the door and got in. Chad was on the phone, facing outside hence when he turned, she motioned to the paper bag in hand with their lunch before she walked to the couch and placed it on the coffee table.

She removed the KFC bucket from the bag and took out the paper plates. Chad walked towards her and sat next to her on the couch, still talking over the phone. He crossed his long legs while PJ gulped down a few breaths. Ok, the man was eye candy.

Chad finished his call and turned to PJ.

"How are you feeling today," he asked her while she smiled and answered, "Great and thanks for everything."

Chad nodded.

"I want to apologize," PJ said. He raised a brow, "Apologize for what?"

"For kicking you out of your bed."

Chad chuckled. He had been startled when she started removing her clothes during the night.

He had flicked his fingers in her face and she wasn't aware of him but merely turned the other side and slept. Chad covered the satiny smooth skinned body with a sheet while fending off the urge of acting like a teenager on heat. He had desperately wanted her and was battling a crazy hard on while she continued snoring away.

He was contemplating shifting to a couch away from temptation when he got kicked out of the bed. He grinned; in future he would tie her legs up, if her habit was kicking while she slept.

"So PJ, let's hear your huge and grand proposal."

PJ choked on her meat while he took a bite on his and handed her a glass of water. After her cough ended and she gratefully finished the water, he spoke, "Relax PJ, am down for you too girl and am flattered."

He grinned and she laughed at the realization that he was joking.

Chad loved her laugh and would have preferred to hear it over and over again. He would never tire of it.

PJ cleared her throat. Chad could see she was about to open that cute mouth and apologize again. He shook his head. "I think you have apologized enough for today."

PJ huffed and he grinned.

She put the paper plate onto the table. "I just need a tiny favor," she said, indicating with her fingers how tiny that favor could be.

He waited for her to continue. "My uncle who also happens to be my boss is having an anniversary tomorrow evening and I was wondering if you could be my date."

Chad stood up and pretended to be in deep thought. "Your date, hmmm. What will I get in return for being your date?"

Her mouth fell open not having anticipated that before she snapped it shut and cleared her throat. She stood up from the couch.

"You will get me."

Ook, she had him, he thought and looked at her before she turned away and whispered, "I mean when you need someone to be your plus one, I will be your girl."

"Hmmm. I still have to think about it, since my future generation might be in trouble where you are concerned."

She bit her bottom lip that managed to spear through to his groin.

"What can I do to make you fast track that thought?" Couldn't the guy see that she was nervous as it was? Chad smiled and walked to where she stood.

He could hear PJ sharply inhale. Guess she was as affected as him. "A kiss will do."

PJ looked trapped for a second like she would flee as her hands shook in the anticipation of running her hands on him once again.

The last time she kissed Chad if only he hadn't said she was a hooker, she would have given it up that night. She was ready to do so. His kiss was passionate and heady, all-consuming managing to make her forget even her surroundings. For that moment, she wanted to remain in his arms and forget everything else and the consequences be damned.

She heaved a long sigh and shifted, having made up her mind to see where this would all lead, stood on her tiptoes before she kissed his cheek and smiled.

"Come on PJ, that can't be a kiss. You want me to be your plus one, I guess so that you mess the mind of that ex of yours meaning in your case it's more than being a date." She gasped.

How did Chad know, then she remembered that he had stood by her door the day she forgot her purse.

He rather looked intimidating, studying her as if waiting for her to give away something. She smiled, well if he wanted this, he was going to get it, instead of shying away from this sexual tension going on, she was going to make sure she enjoyed this kiss.

PJ shifted and stood very close to him before she pulled at the lapels of his jacket. "Ooh, I like the take charge kind of woman," Chad whispered in his deep voice and had her chuckling. "You are not making this any easier for me."

"Ok, I thought I was helping you with a confidence booster."

"Chad,"

"Hmmm,"

"Shut up," she said and huffed as a smile tugged at the corner of his mouth.

Shutting her eyes from the intensity of his, she softly pasted her lips on his warm one in a kiss. That got him moving because he pulled her close and slid his tongue, ooh boy she was in trouble. Her body was already trembling. If she didn't know better this kiss was going to be her ruin for any other man.

Like the first time they met it was passionate as he delved deep and she giggled when their tongues did a mating dance. She moaned; she couldn't help it. The deliciousness of the kiss had melted her bones and her insides had all become liquid.

He must have sensed she would topple over because her legs at the moment wouldn't hold the weight, Chad swiftly picked her up and sat her on the table before he cradled her face in his hands and whispered, "You are beautiful."

PJ grasped his tie and leaned in, smelling the faint spicy aftershave and sweet warm breath. Her body was tingling, longing for his touch. "You too," she whispered and parted her lips as that same current of electricity speared through to her body.

Not satisfied with the desk, Chad picked her up and straddled her long legs over his waist. PJ ran her hand through his hair, moaning as wave after wave of intoxicating pleasure overcame her.

Chad's hand was underneath her chiffon top and was trailing to her breast. He kissed her deeply and at the same time squeezed her breast while she nearly screamed. The scream died down due to the fact he smothered it with another passionate kiss and lightly bit her lip. She could feel his hand on her padded breast as he had skillfully cupped it and was rubbing the nipple and the lacy material adding more of the delicious sensation.

She would have wept that he took her there and then and she knew she would never regret it. She belonged right there in his arms.

A few of her buttons had come loose as Chad for a second drew away and looked appreciatively at her full breasts in the lacy bra. "You are beautiful," he said again. Now that was making her crazy, hearing him say that. This was Chad who had seen her at her worst, and that complement and deep voice had already made her wet for him. Her hands had also been at work because his shirt was out of the jeans.

The door suddenly opened and had both of them pulling away, her trying to button up her top while Chad shielded her with his tall frame.

"Daniels," he gruffly said.

"Sorry Cap, there has been a homicide..." Daniels didn't finish because the captain shooed him with the hand. He nodded and shut the door.

The phone rang. "Did she secure the date," Meghan asked Daniels.

"She secured more than the date. The moans could be heard in the corridor." The sister gasped over the phone while Daniels chuckled.

Chad cleared his throat and turned to PJ. He buttoned the remainder of the buttons on her chiffon top, seeing her hands were shaking like crazy and she wasn't looking at him. After he was done, having tucked his shirt back in, he clutched her hands and kissed them.

"I will be your date."

"Whaa," she appeared to have forgotten what they had been discussing. "On two conditions though," Chad said while PJ raised a delicate brow in question.

"This will be an actual date in which we will both enjoy each other's company; none has to prove anything to anyone else."

Her body was screaming and dancing at the fact that Chad wanted her to be his girl. She tilted her head up, stared into those deep brown eyes and slowly nodded. She could definitely do that.

"Another condition," Chad continued to say. "Let me take the lead. That means my sis will help you get ready for the occasion so you look the part of being my girl."

PJ opened her mouth to protest but Chad shook his head.

"But Chad I can do that on my own."

"PJ, this party that you are having is for the Gilberts right." She nodded her head. "I thought as much. How many people from your office have actually been invited?"

That got her thinking. It had been odd because usually the Gilberts invited all the employees at the firm. But for their upcoming fiftieth anniversary, a few in senior positions had been invited. She on the other hand because she was family. Come to think of it, the gathering was small and intimate, different from usual.

"My parents will be there."

Now she was about to faint. Which meant her date would be...her mind froze. If he were to attend the party as the prince and not the captain, then she had to look the part of a girl worthy of him. She gulped down a few breaths.

Chad caught her trembling hands. "I thought you were not aware, but seeing your reaction tells me otherwise. Meghan told you."

She nodded and shook her head at the same time.

"I hope you don't mind."

Oh please, did she mind going with the prince. Wow, not at all.

"Why should I mind Chad, it's who you are. By the way, how do I address you?"

Chad chuckled, "you are adorable you know that." He leaned in and tenderly kissed her, taking his time. She wound her arms on his neck as the kiss deepened and Chad pulled her close. Gasping at feeling his arousal through the clothes she pulled away.

"Unless you want me to fall flat on my face because my legs can't hold me up, please stop." Chad chuckled and put his hands in his pockets. "On second thoughts," PJ said before she flung herself into his arms.

She opened the door and shut it behind her. Let the prince think about what she had in store for them. She smiled dreamily, thinking back to the passionate kiss they had just shared. She leaned on the door; her legs had become rubber as she had predicted.

"Girl you are a hussy," Daniels commented while she giggled. He was standing in the middle of the corridor.

"I am not."

He rolled his eyes, "you went on a couple of dates with me remember."

She quickly walked to where he stood. "And we agreed to just be friends."

He scoffed.

"So will you be leaving soon?"

"For?"

PJ rolled her eyes, "you mentioned a homicide."

"Oh that. It was an excuse; we could hear your moans and groaning. Sex at the office is a no, no."

PJ shrieked and hit him hard. "Meghan is on the line," he handed her the phone while they walked out of the building.

Chapter 10

"WHERE was your brother before I made the Tony mistake," PJ groaned while Meghan giggled. She had received a full five-star treatment at the spa after their shopping and was now lying, lazing around on the folding chair at the pool. Barb was there shrieking in the pool and making a spectacle of herself as usual.

"My brother was there, you just didn't notice him," Meghan answered while she huffed. "Heard Barb had informed you about the blind date and that's the same time you decided to get into a relationship with Tony."

PJ groaned at the thought, that was the worst mistake she ever made. Her mother didn't even like Tony. She was totally against their relationship and had told her so in that she was selling herself short. Well at that time she was naive and thought her love for him was enough for the both of them. Except Tony didn't love her the way she loved him. They have always had a third party in their relationship.

"So did you talk about anything else, apart from almost making love in his office," Meghan asked while PJ groaned again and shut her eyes.

"This is an actual date; he knows that I know he is a prince that's all."

Meghan sat up, "and nothing else." She looked disappointed when PJ shook her head.

"Was he meant to say something?"

Meghan hesitated before she took a sip of her orange juice and cleared her throat.

"Chad will be going back to Safe Haven with the parents."

"I am sure he didn't mention this since he will be back before I know it"

Meghan took hold of her hands and sadly looked at her. "Chad and I both turned 30 a month ago. As the heir apparent, he had made an agreement with the king that when he turned thirty, he would go back and take up his rightful place. His days of being free to do what he wants are over. Since I heard about how great you were getting along, I thought he might have hinted that to you, that my parents' coming signals the end to his stay here."

PJ gulped down, taking it all in at the same time. She rather felt disquieted. Right when she was getting to enjoy being with someone who understood and liked her, this had to come up.

Meghan smiled. "It would have been wonderful too if he popped the question, therefore having a bride who is used to his lifestyle and way of thinking, than one who would be chosen for him." Her heart had beat thrice at that notion, but she shook her head. "We barely know each other, I doubt."

"You will eventually get to know each other well, but right now it's more about racing against time. If he were to ask you, would you accept my brother PJ, knowing that you will have to leave everyone and everything behind."

Hard questions she had never thought of. Her mother brought her to the States at the age of twelve and she was rather content in visiting Safe Haven. Staying there indefinitely was another thing altogether, especially with her dysfunctional family. They made one think twice.

She hadn't even gone on an actual date with Chad. She almost wept for the lost four years, when she could have pursued a meaningful relationship with someone who loved and put her needs first.

Tony be damned. If Chad asked, she would accept, even if they had just known each other for a month. With Tony it was four but what came out of it, nothing but a pile of ashes.

"I love your brother," she simply answered and realized it to be the truth. She was one person who had never believed in love at first sight but with Chad they appeared to be an exception to that notion. She thought back to when they met.

What crushed her the most wasn't that Tony was marrying her friend, what bothered her to the core and made her drink so she numbed the ache was the handsome stranger who turned out to have a fetish for the ladies of the night.

As much as she hated to admit this, she would have been that for him that day, except she didn't want to settle for less, one-night stands were never ideal. She knew first hand from being with Tony. She caught on some feelings whilst he didn't but kept her on for years.

It's so funny that she had never bumped into Chad before, but after her binge she appeared to bump into him all the time. Time seemed to stop as they would gaze longingly at each other before one or both looked away and PJ dashed like crazy, running away from him and what was happening to her.

Even with the knowledge of him being a prince, she didn't regard the title at all. She would have had him any other way even if he was just her simple captain. Chad was a nice solid guy who would always have her back. Look at the way he had taken care of her in her drunken state the day after her binge before Barb arrived.

She had puked her guts out, while he held her hair and gave her the cold towel before making her lie on the couch. What about the night his niece shoved those peanuts into her mouth? Chad wasn't repulsed but rather joked about it before wrapping his strong arms around her and making her feel special. He even kissed the swollen lips and eyes.

The worst moments in her life when she felt her world was on the verge of crashing down, Chad was able to see her through. Instead of her actions being a turn off to him, he actually wanted to get to know her better.

Well, that part of knowing her better Barb did tell her amidst her long lecture of pointing out on Chad being different from what she was used to.

"Chad dates with the intention of marrying," Barb had said. "So, seeing he has his eyes on you, means you are the girl he will focus on and take the time to know. Unlike Tony, he doesn't have a wandering eye. You are safe with him."

"He sounds like a girl" PJ had said and received a pinch from Barb. PJ liked the girl and she had told her best friend that. Barb had squealed, hugged her almost to the point of cutting her life short by squeezing the breath out of her before rushing to join Meghan in the pool.

That was some thirty minutes back before Meghan joined her on the recliner and hinted too and she told him that she was in love with Chad.

Meghan squeezed her hand. "I am glad to hear that," she commented before she returned to lying back on the recliner.

• • ❧ • •

BY THE TIME THEY WERE ready for the party, PJ was battling between being angry and nervous.

Angry that Chad had called just to hear her voice but didn't mention anything of his imminent departure.

Who was she to get angry anyways? She barely knew him. Then why was it that her heart ached at the thought of him never coming back.

Why was she becoming furious at the fact that he wasn't giving their love a chance? Did it mean he was just going to wow her for this evening and disappear forever? Was she meant to be left with the memory of once having met and been loved by a prince? Did Chad feel the same? Love her too?

She gritted her teeth, if Chad knew what was good for him, he would propose to her as expected.

She huffed and looked at herself in the mirror once again, not believing the haughty, elegant and beautiful woman staring back at her. Meghan sure knew her thing and Chad had been right after all.

In her wildest dreams she wouldn't have chosen the green satiny dress that clung to her body and pooled on her feet to wear to the party. That had been Chad's choice actually. Her hair had been made to perfection. She was no longer the sensibly dressed divorce attorney.

The door slid open. PJ gasped and turned, having caught his reflection in the mirror as he shut the door tightly behind him. Indeed, he was dressed as she had suspected. His tall frame was encased in black trousers that fit him to perfection. And the jacket had gold buttons. Meghan had actually informed her that the jewelry she was wearing was the actual deal, diamonds mined in their kingdom including on Chad's jacket.

What a way of shocking someone to their early grave.

She didn't want to be looking over her shoulder fearing she would be kidnapped. She chuckled at the fact that Meghan had told her to relax after she had commented, "these look like the real thing."

Meghan had raised a delicate brow. "They are sweetie," before she continued to give her the teardrop diamond earrings to wear.

"Whaaa, you can't be serious, I can't go out like this wearing your family fortune."

"It's a good thing" Meghan had answered. "At least we know where you stand where Chad is concerned. He will propose to you."

"How do you know?"

"Like you mentioned, you are wearing the family heirlooms."

"How is it different, Cherise would have worn this."

Meghan had huffed before she touched her by the shoulders. "Cherise was spoiled, cunning and a snob. I think Chad knew deep within hence he never told her. Yes, he bought her designer clothes and bags but when he started cutting off on her spending and reminding her that he was just a cop, it put a damper on the relationship. Let alone she believed that he was sponging on Robin and I, not aware that he is the one who bought the house as a gift for our wedding."

PJ giggled at that.

"The day he proposed the hussy told him his finances were not set, she couldn't marry him."

PJ shook her head, "Chad really dated someone shallow like that." The sister snorted. "My brother is one of those people who loves easily and unconditionally. Don't let his stature make you think otherwise in that he is tough, when he falls it's hard and deep." PJ had blushed at that from the way Meghan had stared at her, having said that. That had been a few hours ago when Meghan said that.

Chad turned and winked at her. His whole stature spoke of pride and nobility. He walked towards her and reached for her hand.

"Chad," PJ whispered, not able to say anything with the intensity in his eyes. He tenderly kissed her. After they drew apart, he whispered, "You take my breath away."

"You too," she whispered back before kissing him with the passion and love she felt.

"Babe is they something that you need to tell me," Chad chuckled while she huffed. His hands had trailed to her butt. She didn't want a hint of a panty line showing, so she had settled to go without. Ok, with the way he was holding her, that had been a mistake. Granny pants were welcome to stop her from acting up on the sexual desires she was having of him.

"Not another word Chadwick Johnson," she weakly threatened as he pulled her close and she caught a whiff of his spicy aftershave while his hands cradled her butt. Boy did he even know what he was doing to her. With the way he winked, he knew. Naughty prince, she thought and ran her hands on his face.

"You clean up well."

He grunted, still wearing a concerned expression on his face.

"I don't know how I should feel"

"About what?"

"The fact that my woman has no panties on. Like you are ready for...."

Chad swore and turned away from her. He limped before he cursed and this time grabbed her and crushed her with a hard kiss as punishment.

He lightly bit her lip and PJ gasped. She couldn't knee him since he had trapped her to the wall with his hard frame pressing against her legs.

"Not this time sweetie," he whispered before he passionately kissed her and she responded back with the same fervor. He picked her up and she was grateful for the slit on the side of the dress as he wrapped her rubbery legs around his waist.

"You don't know what you are doing to me," he said as he bucked his hips and PJs hand trailed to the belt. A knock had them freezing on the spot.

"We will be late you two," Meghan hollered.

PJ slid slowly to the ground and Chad gave her a quick hard kiss. "Tonight, after the party will finish what we started."

PJ blushed at the intensity and promise in his eyes, like he was telling her that this was just the beginning of them not the end.

"My makeup, hair."

She touched her head, fearing their little episode had ruined his sister's efforts. He reached for the box of tissue and removed the lipstick that had gone overboard while she took out another tissue and did the same. Straightened his jacket, he patted her hair, grinned before he turned her to face the mirror with his arms around her. "You are perfect," he whispered in her ear as butterflies fluttered in her tummy and the hairs at the nape rose from his warm breath. They made a rather striking couple.

She looked content actually, a woman in love.

"Shall we?" Chad asked and offered her his arm as she slid her hand in the crook.

"Yes, we shall." She smiled as he led her out of the house to the car waiting for them.

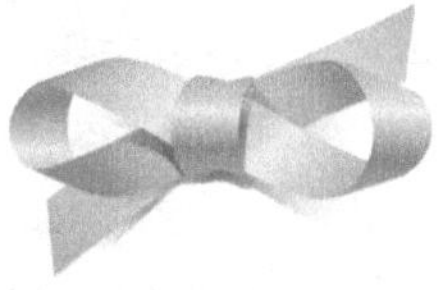

Chapter 11

"HOO, slow down there, your jealousy is beginning to show," Tony said to Cherise who had gulped down another glass of wine while looking at the beautiful couple on the dance floor.

"What about you? Hmmm, aren't you going to take away that girlfriend of yours from my man?"

Tony rolled his eyes and at the same time was trying to get over the shock.

Shaz was sulking lately after having told her he wasn't ready to be a dad, so he had come with a friend of a cousin instead, Cherise. She knew her way around the influential people in society hence would not embarrass him, especially after having caught wind of who would be attending the anniversary.

The Gilberts appeared to know some rather influential people including the king and queen of Safe Haven. Their visit wasn't an official one but rather for friends hence it was being kept on the low-key. The crown prince would also be in attendance. The dark tinted cars had drawn to a halt outside the Gilbert mansion before the doors were opened and the queen glided out after the king.

"Welcome to my humble abode your highness," Mr. Gilbert said before he hugged the King, their easy friendship clearly seen by all. Tony heard a gasp from his date and turned to look at her. Her eyes were round like saucers in astonishment before she pointed out to the prince. He frowned as he wondered if he knew the man. The man reached out to his date. Attractive silky long legs emerged from the car before the lady placed her hand in the prince's and emerged.

Some men were just damn lucky, he thought, waiting to see the face of the lady with the sexy pair of legs. The prince kissed the lady before turning to face where the others were headed. That's when Tony got stunned and his jaw dropped at seeing who the beauty was, hanging on the prince's arm. PJ.

"What the hell," he swore under his breath.

"That's my girlfriend."

Cherise chuckled on his side before she whispered. "She can't be your girl, if she is with him."

Tony took note of the beautiful couple and scowled. Over his dead body would PJ get away with this? She was his woman and didn't belong to anyone else. The prince leaned in to whisper something to her while they walked behind the queen getting into the house. PJ giggled as Tony clenched his hands into a fist.

And to think the woman had been holding out on him, demanding marriage and acting like sleeping with him was a chore. At this moment she didn't look like one who dreaded sex, but rather those smoky eyes spoke volumes to her date. He huffed.

"And then," Cherise asked.

"You worry about that man getting his filthy hands off my girl, I heard you are rather good at seducing men," he snarled.

Cherise smiled, gritting off the snide comment she was about to make. He was right on one point though.

"Thought you said PJ was a log in bed, that's why you always cheated on her, if Chad has a thing for her, no need to worry then. He will tire of her pretty soon," Cherise said. Their sex life had actually been phenomenal. That's one thing she missed about Chad, except she was too greedy and liked money more. She took a glass of wine from a waiter once they were inside the house and gulped it down, having second thoughts on her hasty decision.

Chad was the crown prince, her mind sang. And to think she refused his marriage proposal. Well, that will definitely be rectified.

One thing she knew about her man is that he was faithful to a fault and didn't move on easily meaning he still loved her. The woman on the side was nothing compared to her. Look at her, laughing with the queen like they were old friends. She should be the one standing there, talking to the queen and being by Chad's side. She huffed when Chad and his date walked to the dance floor and swayed to the beat of music.

Grabbing for another glass and contemplating on how to have one minute with Chad to convince him that she was ready, she rolled her eyes when Tony remarked, "Whoa, slow down there, your jealousy is beginning to show. I hate women who cause scenes."

"Even if I managed to get Chad away from her, what would you say to PJ," Cherise asked. She looked at Tony from above the rim of the glass. "You do that darling and we'll both be happy by the outcome. I have my ways. Despite how it looks PJ will always be mine," Tony smirked and grabbed a drink too, already contemplating the end of the short-lived romance playing out in front of him.

They had done that in their four years together too. PJ almost left him for good but she always came back. He looked ahead, maybe this time it might be different, seeing how carefree she looked. To hell, he thought, he still had an ace up his sleeve.

PJ was in awe having been introduced to Chad's parents immediately when they got into the huge hall at her uncle's place. One glance at her had the queen hugging her instead with a catch in her breath and a few tears shed after she heard her name. She wondered at the queen's reaction before she curiously looked at Chad who winked in return.

Was she missing out on something vital here? She could get it if it was about Chad proposing but not what she had witnessed. The queen had hugged her like a long-lost friend. "Shall we dance," Chad asked. The queen nodded at them before they walked to the dance floor.

Chad leaned closer and whispered, "Did I mention that you look beautiful today." She giggled, "Yes a million times." He twirled her around before she went back into his arms. They danced silently together for a while before PJ asked, "Is something bothering you"

Chad frowned. "I'm still concerned over your lack of panties. I know I mentioned that we will be attending this party as a couple, but isn't it too fast to be going without panties, this is our first date."

"I am really going to knee you in front of everyone now," PJ whispered while he chuckled. "And there I was thinking you had more pressing matters bothering you than my pantie-less state."

"Well, you have to admit it's distracting."

"Ya it is especially if you keep on running your hands," she scowled and released a small gasp before she reached for his hand and slid it back onto the small of her back not the lower side he was hovering at. "I am not your wife and you are already taking liberties sir."

"We can rectify that right at this moment. The thought of you dressing like a hooker, getting drunk and going without your panties is meant for me and no one else. Shall we tell my parents that you agreed?"

He groaned and pulled her closer after she stepped on his leg with her heeled foot, digging deep and nearly making him cry out. "Then there is this habit of yours of always resorting to violence."

"How do you expect me to react when you assume everything? What did I agree to?"

He twirled her around before she came back into his arms. "Meet me upstairs in the guest room after ten minutes so we go over your agreement." He winked and kissed her quickly before someone cleared their throat behind them, it was her uncle. Chad smiled and nodded to the uncle before he walked away.

"Happy anniversary uncle G." PJ said as they started dancing.

"Thank you dear." Her uncle smiled at her. "By the way, when did you meet Chad? My dear girl, you have started hiding things from me."

She smiled, wondering where to begin from.

"I am happy that you finally let go of Tony."

"What makes you sure about that?"

"The love in your eyes for Chad. Mmhmm, it's that obvious," he nodded when she gaped her mouth open in shock.

"I have never believed in fate, until today," her uncle said.

"What are you talking about?"

"Your mother was unhappy in her marriage and her greatest regret was that she got married out of duty rather than love."

PJ nodded, she had always known that story since her parents ended up separating and her mom left Safe Haven with her. She had been twelve years old at the time.

"Your mother wanted something different for you. She didn't want you to have an unhappy marriage like her and hence decided to give you the freedom to choose your love. Coming here would not only give you the independence that you would never have experienced at Safe Haven, but you would have a choice on how to live your life."

PJ would never forget the night before they left. How her parents had argued when her mother discovered about his affair and love child. On the other hand, it was a known fact that PJs marriage would be arranged too. Her life had been planned out and she wouldn't have a say in that matter.

"She despaired when you fell in love with Tony. Blamed herself that she shouldn't have given you the freedom." Her uncle chuckled while PJ nodded since he was telling her what she knew already. The last straw to her one-sided love was when she caught Tony with Shaz, a week after when she traveled back to the States after her mother's funeral.

While she mourned her mother's death, Tony had been having his fun. Just like her mother didn't like him, Tony didn't respect her memory. PJ moved out that same day from Tony's apartment and moved in with her former roommate and best friend Barb while Shaz, her childhood friend and confidant, moved into Tony's apartment, unrepentant over having been caught.

Two weeks after the incident, she met Chad. PJ sighed as her uncle tilted her chin to look at her. "That's in the past now, I am happy that you and Chad found each other."

They danced silently for a while. "By the way your mother never mentioned the man you were matched with."

PJ shook her head while her uncle chuckled before he grinned widely and stated simply, "It was Chad."

"It can't be," PJ stared at him in astonishment. "I am as overwhelmed as you dear. That's the reason why I said, I've never believed in fate till today."

The queens' reaction suddenly made sense.

"Now can I fire Tony from the firm?"

PJ opened her eyes wide before it suddenly dawned on why her uncle kept him on. He feared Tony might hurt her by taking out his frustrations on her. She had held onto her one-sided love while her family worried and feared for her. If her uncle had done something to Tony, she would have disowned the very family that loved her, that's how blind she was.

"I am sorry for having put you through all that," she muttered under her breath.

"I am glad you came to your senses before it was too late. Your mother is surely looking down upon you with pride. My sister can now rest in peace knowing she never destroyed your life by going against the norm. You have grown to be a beautiful, self-assured young woman and you will one day make a great queen."

"Oh uncle." PJ almost sobbed when she heard him say that. She wouldn't be rushing things with Chad after all. They had a lifetime of getting to know each other since theirs had been a match that was made long back. Maybe that was the reason why those other relationships they had been in flopped and never worked out.

"PJ don't you think you have danced for long enough with my husband?" her aunt spoke. PJ stepped away and took her aunt's hand before placing it in her uncles. The aunt winked and mouthed, "He is waiting for you."

So, everyone in the family knew that Chad was proposing tonight. She watched the two people she loved dance and hoped that she and Chad would share this kind of bond and love till their death. Heaving in a deep breath and slowly exhaling, she walked out of the hall and climbed up the stairs to where Chad was, waiting for her.

Chapter 12

Chad paced the room running the words he would say in his mind. PJs family had been more than helpful, including preparing a small heaven for them in the room he would pop the question in. The aunt had flagged her hands before stating, "You kids of nowadays look at love differently, and I don't have to expect you to be chaste with each other so I am preparing this for your night."

Chad had schooled his expression while the woman went on to scatter some flower petals on the bed. He glanced at his watch and opened the velvet box with the engagement ring. This time he would rather ask the woman alone than put her on the spot and get the Cherise reply.

He chuckled as he thought about the fact that PJ would never act like Cherise, they were different. Practice makes perfect, he thought before he knelt down on the carpeted floor and recited his speech.

"I know we have only known each other for a short while but I feel that we have known each other for a lifetime." That sounded corny, so he decided to use another tactic. Heaving a sigh, he cleared his throat and whispered, "From the day I met you, I felt drawn to you. A lot of things went through my mind, but one thought remained at the forefront, how I wanted you. Knowing you has been like a roller-coaster ride that I don't want to end. I love you PJ with all of my heart. Make me the happiest man by accepting me to be your husband. I promise to love and cherish you always. You will never regret this. Already we have lost so many years apart and I feel if I don't ask you now, I will forever regret not having done so."

He drew in a deep breath and stood up.

"I will marry you Chad," he heard a voice say as he turned around and found Cherise standing at the door.

He frowned. Cherise shut the door quickly and walked further into the room. "Hey baby," she greeted before she rushed into his arms. Chad didn't move. Cherise looked up and smiled. "I have missed you."

That finally had Chad move as he shifted away from her. "What are you looking for here?" She giggled, "Is that the way to greet your girl."

Chad scowled, "Didn't you decide that I wasn't good enough for you."

"Oh that," she waved her hand dismissively. "You can't blame a girl for wanting security, Chad. I thought you were not ready for marriage, but I see you are. Why didn't you tell me you were a prince, I would have accepted on the spot when you asked? Baby I have missed you and I want you back."

She ran her hands on his face and smiled at him. "Don't you miss us Chad," she asked and drew him for a kiss.

PJ gasped when she witnessed the kiss and almost yelled and plodded into the room ready for a fight. Not this time, Chad was hers and that hussy would know soon enough. She was dragged from the door and her voice muffled as a hand covered it. The door got shut behind her before she whirled around, angry at the intruder.

"Tony," she huffed.

"Hey baby, as you can see Chad is making out with his real girlfriend, the one he wants to spend the rest of his life with."

"Are you joshing with me now?" She yelled and turned to leave the room. "I knew you would say that, don't be foolish darling, that lover of yours will cast you aside once he found out what you have been up to."

PJ frowned. This was silly and Tony knew it.

He grinned before he stated, "I wonder if the people will accept a future queen who has spurned their laws and traditions. Safe Haven is still primitive in that regard in case you forgot baby."

Seeing PJ now stood frozen on the spot, Tony knew he had already won. He walked towards her and whispered, "Now let me tell you a little story babe. I think you will like it as much as I do."

.. ❧ ..

"THE YOUNG LADY LEFT with her boyfriend," Mary said while the uncle choked. Chad had come downstairs a while ago looking for PJ. After making himself clear to Cherise and driving her home before she made a scene, all he had wanted was to propose to his love without any interruptions except PJ was no longer there. The party had ended a few minutes ago and the guests left without any sign of her. Her phone was not reachable and kept on going to voicemail while her best friend Barb said she hadn't seen her.

"It can't be true, there has to be a huge misunderstanding."

"Mr. Gilbert, you know how crazy PJ is for Tony. She must have gone back to him again" Mary said, adding more fuel to the fire, not aware of the impact her words were having on everyone.

She could swear PJ had really left with Tony. She saw them using the kitchen door, away from everyone. She suspected that maybe the reason why PJ hadn't announced this time that she was back with Tony was because of such a reaction from her uncle.

Chad curled his hand into a fist while Mr. Gilbert bellowed for Mary to stop spewing nonsense. Chad unfurled his hands and reached out to the old man, understanding in his eyes. Maybe he had been wrong and was rushing this whole proposal thing, besides what Mary was saying wasn't new to him since a colleague at her worksite once pointed out that aspect about PJ and Tony. He had been such a fool and got carried away into thinking she would never go back. "It's ok sir. I understand" Chad managed to say.

"No, you don't, my prince, for the first time she seemed happy with you. She was looking forward to your proposal and came upstairs to look for you." Chad frowned. Could PJ have witnessed him and

Cherise and concluded the worst. He unloosened his tie. He needed to explain to her fast. His phone vibrated and he answered it without checking the caller id. "Chad."

It was PJ.

"Baby," he whispered, "where are you, everyone is worried about you," he said.

"I need time Chad," is all she said before she hung up.

Chad sat on the couch. Guess she had made her decision after all. "We should go," he said to his parents while his mother looked at him with concern. Standing up again with all the willpower he could muster, he hugged her uncle and aunt. "Thank you for everything."

"What did she say," the uncle asked.

"Do not worry, she is fine," Chad said. His heart was tearing into a million pieces and he couldn't be in the same room with these people who were looking at him with concern and sympathy. He walked out of the house with his mother calling out after him.

Chapter 13

"**Y**OUR highness, Miss Edwina has arrived."

Chad nodded to his butler before he turned and faced the window. It had been a month since he left the States and his memories of PJ behind. He wondered if she was happy. Though she had disappointed him, he still hoped for the best for her. He heaved a weary sigh and walked out of the study.

He managed to get hold of Barb before he left the States and gave her the plane ticket for PJ. He also sent a voice note on her voicemail since she was no longer picking her phone but would quickly be diverted to her voice mail instead. In it, he confessed his love to her.

He hoped she would turn up at the airport the day he left. Seeing PJ not turning up told him everything. She had made her decision. Hence his mother had been rather insistent that he moved on with his life. Didn't his family ever tire in telling him that?

Edwina quickly scrambled to her feet when he came into the drawing room and curtsied. How he hated that. "My prince" she whispered before he nodded for her to take a seat.

"Where is your chaperone," he asked while the young lady flinched. She was cowering again. And there he had been thinking that things had changed back home.

The girls his mother had set him up with were barely in their twenties and cowered at his every word and movement. Edwina for some reason reminded him of PJ. She was beautiful and tall but appeared not to be confident in that fact.

Edwina didn't look him in the eye but rather looked at a distant point on his shoulder. "You asked for me," a voice asked from behind him that had Edwina pasting a genuine beautiful smile on her face while Chad tried to wrap his mind around the fact that he had heard PJs voice.

"I am her chaperone," she said and raised a daring delicate brow. She was dressed in a long sleeved long brown dress with a black belt cinched over her tiny waist. The dress actually couldn't hide the wide hips despite the effort put in. She had the most atrocious glasses perched on her delicate nose and Chad almost laughed. Well right at the moment he felt like throttling that long neck.

"What are you wearing?" he asked in horror.

"Oh these," she lightly touched the reading glasses instead. "My step mother insisted that I look the part of being my young sis chaperone, so to accessorize on the ugly dress, I wore these."

He chuckled while Edwina's eyes widened like saucers at their exchange.

Did they know each other? she curiously looked at both of them. PJ didn't mention anything though. It's not like they shared intimacies but right now she was the one getting confused. PJ never liked Safe Haven and only visited for a short while.

Everyone was surprised when she turned up two days back out of the blue and claimed she needed a rest from her hectic lifestyle. The ever-present boyfriend wasn't there. Come to think of it, he happened to have not been there for the funeral too. How Edwina hated PJs boyfriend. He always made her feel uncomfortable and to make matters worse, her mother liked him.

She had caught them chatting twice or was it thrice and acting like long lost friends. She frowned at that thought.

"So, I heard," PJ removed the glasses, wiped them before placing them back on. "That you are on the lookout for the future queen of Safe Haven."

Chad groaned but was surprised when she smiled and walked towards him. He shifted and settled down, fearing she would knee him on his groin.

"I am happy that you are doing so."

"You are happy," Chad parroted and nearly cursed for sounding like that. He should be the one being offended and not being on the defensive, since she left him a month ago and never tried to get in touch with him.

He cleared his throat and motioned for her to take a seat.

"I think Edwina might make a beautiful queen, don't you think so?" he asked and lightly touched Edwina's shoulder. The girl looked like she would suffocate as she held her breath.

"Breathe" he whispered and gave his full attention to the sister.

PJ almost retorted and removed Chad's hands from her sister. She had been relieved when she found out that Chad wasn't with Cherise. She was a fool, for having thought different when she caught sight of him leaving with Cherise. Tony whispered in her ear, *you see, he has always loved Cherise and you were just a passing fancy.*

That night her phone suddenly went missing and she ran away to her sanctuary as she would usually do when confronted with such situations. It was too weeks after Chad had left, when she got back into the city that Barb gave her the ticket and an apologetic Sharon produced the phone. Apparently, she and Tony had a fall out of some sort. She would have whooped in glee at Sharon's misfortune but she didn't. They had both been victims of loving the wrong person.

She didn't know where her friendship with Shaz stood though. Even if she had forgiven her, she just wasn't ready to pretend that everything was okay.

So much had happened in such a short time that she couldn't take back. She gulped down a few breaths and mumbled. "Yes indeed" before she took the task of pouring the tea into their cups while a stilted silence followed after her answer.

The moment she arrived in Safe Haven, her step mother had been taken aback and was rather posing a lot of questions on why she was there.

Jeez call it her womanly instincts, but her step mother appeared to not like her being there. That was until she heard what was happening. The prince was searching for a bride. Her step mother being aware of the arrangement feared PJ might take her rightful place and fulfill the agreement.

PJ just wasn't in the mood of running up a pricey hotel bill when her father had a huge roof and soft warm bed that had always been hers in the house, that would be too much wastage and all because her step mother deemed her a threat.

"Don't worry step mother, I am not going to destroy your dreams of having the King as your in-law and am with Tony after all."

"Ooh Tony, yes dear, how is he doing since you didn't come with him this time?" She had chuckled nervously while PJ asked instead, "Is Edwina happy about being paraded in front of the prince with the other girls."

"That's silly. How could she not be? It's an honor for her to have been selected."

"What about love?"

"Edwina thinks with her head. Look what your heart has given you so far. No ring on that finger," her step mother had snappishly replied, taking PJ aback while she looked pointedly on her finger before she left. How PJ so hated her attitude, her step mother could be hot and cold at the same time, leaving her to wonder. Surprisingly she had demanded for PJ to chaperone her young sister instead since she was not on the runner up for the future queen position and insisted on the ugly dress.

Wow, PJ rather pitied Chad at the moment and what he had to go through in order to secure his bride. If her step mother was taking such drastic measures, what more the rest of the mothers whose daughters had been selected too.

"Do you know each other," Edwina asked and looked at the prince and her sis.

"Absolutely not, where would we have met and we are lying right through our teeth," both answered in unison while Edwina laughed.

PJ cleared her throat, "We met today in the corridor. Ch...The prince explained how nervous you've been in his company before and wanted you to be open with him. Look at you, he can now see the beautiful young woman you are instead of a shy girl not ready for marriage."

Edwina nervously laughed when PJ said that. She was just as terrible as her mom in match making her with the prince. And there she had been thinking she had finally found an ally. She sighed and continued to give her full attention to the prince as she was expected to, answering everything he asked of her. She could as well imagine what the girls in Esther's time might have felt like. Their kingdom was no different. Well, she wanted to choose her own love but that wasn't going to happen seeing her sister was slowly sipping at the tea and being off course the good chaperone, including telling the prince about her hobbies.

"Excuse me, I need the lady's," PJ said and stood up from the chair before she walked out of the room. She nearly cursed when she stood in the corridor wondering where to go next. Opening one of the doors, she got in and checked if it had a private bathroom. To her relief it did. She opened the tap and splashed water on her face. *I can do this*, she muttered before splashing more water on her face.

Oh hell, I can't, she whispered to her reflection in the mirror. Everything she had convinced herself while in the States, flew out of the window the moment she caught sight of Chad. Tony was right in one aspect. She and Chad could never be together.

Here the laws were stricter and he wasn't her ordinary captain but a prince. She gasped when the door opened and she caught sight of Chad through the mirror.

"My prince." She closed the tap, turned and lowered her eyes. Chad huffed, before he approached her and tilted her head. Reaching out to the towel on the rail he remarked, "Don't you start acting like the women around here," while he dabbed the excess water off her face.

PJ giggled and took the towel from him. There wasn't a need for him to be dabbing her face and any part of her body. Her body quivered at the nearness as she felt his warmth emanating from his being. "How should I act?" she asked, mentally scrubbing off every thought and focusing on the present.

"Like the PJ I know, who kicks me around."

"I thought you didn't like violence."

"With you I can make an exception."

She smiled and cleared her throat before throwing the towel in the basket and walking away from the bathroom.

"My young sis must be waiting for us," she muttered.

"She is not, Michael is entertaining her."

Chad stopped PJ by holding her hand before she could open the door and walk out.

"Have you started avoiding me again?"

"No Chad it's not that."

"What is it then," he asked and watched her chew her bottom lip. He groaned at the action as it managed to spear the groin region making him crazy like before. He wanted her, that's what was at forefront ever since they met. Leaning in, he kissed those sweet plump lips. PJ moaned and kissed him, not holding anything back. She responded with the same fervor.

Reaching out to the jacket, she helped him from it before they continued kissing passionately.

"I have missed you baby," Chad whispered, eliciting a shiver down her spine while her tummy quivered with a flurry of butterflies because of his deep seductive voice. Funny they never slept together but it felt like they knew each other more deeply than any ordinary couple. Chad easily picked her up in one fluid motion and walked towards the bed.

PJ looked so beautiful and her mesmerizing eyes beckoned for him to discover more about her, he thought before he lay next to her.

"Are you sure about this?" For a second PJ was taken aback. Why would she not be sure? Had Tony been talking with him about her misgivings and insecurities?

No this was different. Chad was different from Tony in that their life had already been planned out before they even met. She belonged to Chad and she couldn't run away from that startling truth. PJ ran her hand on his face instead and smiled. "I've missed you, sorry for leaving you..." she didn't get to finish because Chad placed his finger on her lips and shook his head. "You are here now, that's what counts" he said before kissing her. He rolled over her and swore when he reached under her dress.

"Panty's woman," he groaned while she giggled. "This is our second meeting,"

"Actually forth, PJ retorted and flicked her fingers in explanation; there is the moment in the alley, your office and your place. So, I guess now you can't nail me for not wearing any. I didn't want any delays."

"Are you trying to tell me you came all the way expecting this?"

"Of course, we never finished the conversation in the States."

Chad chuckled; she was crazy he thought before he went on to show her how crazy he could be too.

Chapter 14

PJ stirred and opened her eyes. She shifted away from Chads' arms and faced him, looking at his handsome face while he slept. She leaned in to kiss him, giving into the temptation.

Her body was humming at the love making she had experienced. Surprisingly she wanted more of him. She searched deeply in her heart for that guilty voice coming in play but heard nothing. Either she was hardened or this was right.

Chad groaned in response and drew her closer, taking her by surprise.

"Thought you were sleeping," she breathlessly commented after they had drawn apart

"I was until you woke me up with that sweet mouth of yours and silky legs." He ran his hand on her back while her body quivered again in response. Their bodies intertwined; she could feel him getting aroused again.

PJ looked at the clock and abruptly left the bed before she got carried away, "It's getting late, Edwina will start getting worried."

"Relax, like I said Michael is entertaining her. They went shopping and for a movie. I asked for four hours since we need to talk about ourselves."

"What about?"

PJ grabbed her dress that had been carelessly thrown on the chair in the heat of the moment. Chad also woke up while PJ gasped at his well-toned body that was giving her a hard time in trying to stop her fingers from tracing those contours on his torso. He looked at her, daring her to comment while her mouth suddenly went dry.

He winked then did something that made her chuckle at the same time she found arousing. He moved his chest, flexing the muscles.

"Like what you see," he asked

"Put on your clothes man," she finally said and threw his trousers at him.

"What if I don't want to? What if I want to remain in bed with you today?"

"Well, that can't happen. You have a dinner party at eight. You have still got to select your bride."

"My bride is you," Chad said calmly and reached to her before pulling her into his lap.

PJ giggled and pushed him away, fighting off the temptation to return back to bed before she reached out for one of the shoes under the bed and wore it.

"That's silly, I am not suitable and you know it."

Chad frowned. "What are you talking about?"

Seeing she wasn't going to fulfill his desire of lazing in bed, he reached for his shirt and wore it.

"In case you didn't notice, there is no spot of blood on your sheets."

"And what has that got to do with being my bride."

PJ rolled her eyes. "The future queen of Safe Haven is meant to be pure."

"That's madness," Chad said and reached out to hug her, nuzzling her neck while her body trembled in response. "Those things are ancient; they don't apply to any of us."

PJ reluctantly left the comfort of his arms. It was now or never. Chad had to be practical in this, just like she was about to be practical.

"Says who, Chad the man who grew up in the States or Chad the prince."

"My parents like you and I love you PJ."

PJ shut her eyes, the ache in her heart setting in again. The insults Tony had thrown her way. What a fool she had been.

"No Chad, I can't be your bride."

Chad's expression changed. She could literally feel him withdrawing and the warmth in him cooling down. That wasn't her intention.

"So, what is this that is going on here? Is this some kind of game to you?" The calmness in his voice and bleak look had her thinking of a calm before a storm. It was never good. She walked to the window, not wanting to look at his face.

"It's not a game. Chad I can be all this but never your wife."

"Can you hear yourself?"

He furiously walked around the bed and reached towards his pair of trousers after wearing his briefs before he yanked them on, hating the sound of the words she was spewing. What was wrong with her?

"PJ," he walked to where she stood and held her by the shoulders after he was done with dressing. She wasn't looking at his eyes. In the short time he had known her; he knew what she was thinking when she looked at him.

"PJ baby, look at me," he coaxed and kissed her. Her eyes flew open.

"What the hell," he swore under his breath. Whatever had happened after the night she left was serious and haunting her?

"What are you hiding from me PJ," he asked. She turned away. "Nothing Chad."

"You can't tell me that it's nothing." He pulled her back to face him. "I thought I would never ask about that night but now I need to know more than ever, did you really go back to Tony."

Her lip quivered as if she was about to cry. "Chad you are hurting me," she whispered.

He let her arms go when it suddenly dawned that he'd clutched onto her hard.

"I am sorry," he said contritely and this time audibly swore when for the first time he saw a flash of fear. It was instant and he thought he had imagined it.

"You don't think I would hurt you." PJ swallowed hard before she slowly shook her head. Shit

Tony must have hurt her before. Why didn't he see that? Was he now blackmailing her too? Is that the reason she didn't want them to be together?

Her mouth thinned. "I don't want to talk about it. What we have on the other hand is not anything unique from what our ancestors..."

She never got to finish because Chad had turned away from her and was putting on his jacket. He looked mighty pissed and not in the mood to listen to what she had to say.

"If you are contemplating the rubbish that I am thinking, don't even voice it out. I will not allow you to degrade our love like this," he ground out. "I am not going to settle for this. It's either I have you or none of you and in no uncertain terms will I fight a ghost from your past."

PJ gasped.

"Michael will drive you and your sister back home," Chad continued before he left with the door banging loudly behind him. PJ slumped onto the bed and wept.

. . ⚬ . .

"YOU LOOK TERRIBLE," was the first thing her step mother said when they got back home. Edwina chuckled and stated "PJ had a terrible headache, so she remained at the palace while I went shopping and watched a movie with the prince."

Adele clapped her hands in delight while PJ looked at Edwina in astonishment. She was insinuating that she went with Chad not Michael, his young brother, well that's what her mother would think from her statement.

"I will come and tell you all about it mama," Edwina said. "Let me assist PJ to bed."

The mother flapped her arms dismissively while PJ marveled at how her young sister had handled the matter of her puffy eyes.

"You owe me," Edwina said once they were in PJ's room.

"Owe you for what," she snorted, "lying to your mother by implying that you went with Chad."

"For the fact that I did not tell mama that you already know Prince Chadwick and you are lovers."

"What gives you that idea?" PJ wearily asked and sat on her bed. Her young sister rolled her eyes. "I am not blind. Mama thinks you are still with Tony but I gather from what I witnessed today that you and the prince did come across each other and fell in love. My question though is how come you are not together."

PJ reached out to the glass of water near the bed and took a sip at it. A headache was slowly setting in and now she had to deal with her smart assed young sister.

"I don't know what makes you think that but that's absurd, like we mentioned. We met in the corridor," PJ managed to say.

Edwina shrugged, "What is absurd is you being on the defensive and denying what can be clearly seen a mile away. You and the prince are lovers. I am not going to pry on what happened after Michael took me out. But please do inform mama so she stops matchmaking me with him. Your prince is way older and worldly. I am not interested but I have to go through this whole dressing up stuff to preserve the family name," she huffed and stomped out of the room banging the door behind her.

PJ lay on the bed and massaged her forehead. Now she had two people who were being impossible in her life. What more would be revealed during the course of days to follow. She bit her hand, muffling the sound of a sob as tears slid down her face.

· · ⚬ · ·

CHAD WAS STILL ANGRY with PJ. How could she degrade herself to being a concubine? God, did such a thing exist even in their century? Yes, it was in the form of a mistress but he didn't want to think about that.

His forefathers might have taken one wife and had those but one was enough for him. If his great grandfather up to his father could do that, he definitely could and no smart assed loose screwed woman could tell him otherwise.

He stared at PJ again and nearly groaned. Sweet Jesus, what was going on in that mind of hers? He could tell she was miserable but her mind made up at the same time. He had planned an outing with her sister just to goad her to reason.

Edwina and Michael had popped into the cake shop to get a treat while they waited for them outside. This had also given Chad the chance to look around the town. His father had surely made some changes as new state of art buildings appeared to have been built during the course of the years he had been away. He wondered if that could be said in the worst of the neighborhoods and made a mental note to pay a visit to them.

"PJ," someone called, waved at her before she crossed the street. The lady smiled at Chad then pulled PJ on the side. Chad chuckled, if he knew women well, then the lady was there to milk for information. He pretended not to be listening to what they were talking about.

"I can't believe this is you. Have you been avoiding me?"

"What makes you say that, Shannon." The woman looked at her from head to toe. "The fact that you haven't visited my home ever since you came back like you usually do."

"As you can see, I have been a bit busy."

The woman shrugged. "Ok, if you say so. How's my little sis Sharon, I haven't heard from her in a while." PJ gulped down a few breaths she had been holding back. Of all people to bump into she hadn't expected to meet one of Shaz relations. *Shaz is pregnant with my ex-boyfriend's baby*, her mind screamed while she said instead, "She is doing great. I will give her a call and demand that she calls you." Shannon giggled but PJ still felt like she was under scrutiny. Shannon had that stare that would make one feel like they are exposed. Shannon smiled in resignation and commented, "You are looking great and girl you are rocking those wide hips."

PJ chuckled absent mindedly and remarked, "It must have been the birth control."

Chad nearly laughed at the horrified expression because PJ noticed her blunder and gasped before she fell into a fit of coughs and flagged her hands dismissively. Chad patted her back and cut in, "What PJ means is that she has had too much of the genetically modified foods."

Shannon's brow was raised at the display of the prince patting PJ's back and shook her head, deciding not to read much into what was happening before she smiled. It was silly of her to think there was anything going on between them, when PJ had Tony in her life. Shaz would usually talk about her best friend's love life and on how she longed to have such a man in her life. According to Shaz, Tony was a good man.

"Is that so, I have heard that it's rare to find natural organic foods overseas. Don't worry, now you can eat healthy to your heart's content."

"I have already started on the regime," PJ mumbled while Shannon giggled. "It's been nice seeing you again," she said before she hugged PJ and walked away from them at a fast pace.

"You didn't need to say that, you know. I didn't need saving."

"Are you sure about that? I thought you would choke from your coughing fit. Besides, do you want the whole kingdom to start talking about the fact that Mr. James' first born daughter is on birth control without being wed, and then they speculate over the man?"

"That's why I don't like staying here for long; everyone is always up in someone's business. Since you are here, why don't you offer free courses of some sort to all people so they mind their business? Gossip should be a punishable offense. You only have to order *off with her head* and it's sorted. No gossiping."

Chad chuckled at that. She definitely was in one of those moods, he thought as she ran her eyes around. Was she uncomfortable being around him? He looked to where his security stood, further apart from them but near enough if something happened.

People were smiling up to them but not coming any closer. He hadn't thought about that part of his life being uncomfortable for her. He sighed and motioned for them to start walking. Edwina and Michael were taking longer in buying that treat. If he didn't know better, he, like PJ, was being relegated to being a guardian while his young brother courted Edwina. The grin had been a dead giveaway when he suggested he took her out the day PJ visited the palace.

"Speaking about birth control, yesterday we didn't, are you sure you are not having a bun in the oven already?"

Chad knew he was pushing it but smothered a laugh at the glare he received from PJ.

She whirled around and angrily answered, "I am not, I am on birth control."

"The woman doth protest too much," he joked while PJ huffed.

"If I didn't know better, I would think there is a bun, that's why the unstable emotions and impractical solutions."

She flared her arms. "You know what, you are impossible. I need the ladies," she said before she walked away from him. Chad chuckled and winked at his security before he yawned and stated, "Women." That had them laughing.

Chapter 15

"I hate you right now," Edwina whispered in PJ's ears while they stood outside the hospital.

"Don't you think it's rather harsh to say those words?" Her young sister rolled her eyes. "Why aren't you coming clean with mama so that I can live my life?"

"Not that again," PJ shut her eyes briefly and heard Edwina huff under her breath before she walked away from her.

PJ looked at the politician who was still making a speech over the opening of a new wing at the Hospital. She sighed. Her feet hurt from standing and her back ached. Edwina was now standing with the rest of the girls so she decided to slip away for a while. Walking to the public wards of the hospital, PJ was taken aback at seeing the deplorable condition. As usual, the prince was being shown the best parts.

"Sorry, Miss, this wing has been shut down for a while," a nurse hurriedly walked to her and said in a bland tone.

"What do you mean shut down, are you implying that patients have taken an off day from being sick and aren't being attended to."

The nurse frowned. "As you are aware, the prince is opening a new wing." PJ waved her hand dismissively. "I need to meet with the person in charge. Tell them Prince Chadwick's manager needs to talk to them urgently." The nurse's eyes widened at the title and she stiffly nodded before she walked away. PJ sighed in relief as the nurse had looked scared when she heard the name but didn't question her further on her bluff. PJ managed to have a chat with the medical services officer and donated some much-needed beds.

"The prince will help out with whatever is needed too. Am sure the beds that have been used in the private wards can be shifted to the older wings than be kept in the storage rooms," she pointed out while the manager frowned at her taking over everything.

His bid to please the lady had made him blurt out that they were actually beds not in use after they refurbished the old private wards.

"Just because the prince advocated for free medical treatment for everyone in the nation, it doesn't make sense why you should drop the standards because of that."

"Don't you think you presume too much," the manager finally blurted out. "If it were not for the fact that I know your father, I wouldn't have listened to you."

The nurse had been agitated but he was beginning to think Miss James had merely thrown the prince's name around to get his attention.

PJs mouth thinned on that notion. That was the reason why things didn't change in the kingdom. With men who thought women couldn't bring up a good idea to make the world a better place.

"Whatever needs to be done, do it." A voice was heard from the door that had the manager gasping and scrambling to his feet from behind his desk.

"Prince Chadwick," the manager greeted.

Chad was leaning on the door. PJ fanned her face at how handsome he looked even at this moment when he wasn't even smiling. She nearly groaned, thinking of how she had thrown his name around to get things moving.

Chad walked further into the room before he settled next to her, while PJ contemplated running for cover. He grasped her hand before she could stand and shook his head. Turning to look at the manager, he frowned and could see the manager squirming on his seat. Whatever it was that he had done was making him uncomfortable in his presence.

"Where are the patients?" He asked. The manager gulped down a few breaths.

"They were referred to other clinics so they wouldn't be a disturbance to your grand opening."

Chad thoughtfully nodded. "And what's the main purpose of a hospital?"

This time the manager swallowed hard and reached for his handkerchief in the pocket before he wiped the sweat on his forehead. He had expected the prince just like any of the royals to open a wing and leave without wandering around the whole of the hospital. Usually, the royals only took a few pictures, cut the ribbon and left for other engagements.

This was all because of this meddlesome lady why the prince had paid a visit to his office. He stretched his collar.

"As for Miss Peggy James, she is not presuming anything by saying that I can help or exerting any rights she is not meant to. She is my manager and she has every damn right."

The manager inhaled sharply at the tone before he slowly nodded. He looked to the door and was relieved that they weren't an audience witnessing all this.

"Miss Peggy James will check on the progress within twenty-four hours, if nothing has been done by then, I would like an accounting on what happened to the two million dollars that was donated. I believe when renovations were proposed, the public wings were also included on the plans. How did you put it, state of the art wards for the common folks?"

PJ smothered a laugh and pitied the manager who was pulling at his collar. Mr. Robert the manager dabbed on the sweat on his mouth and forehead before he grunted since Chad was still staring at him.

"Open the doors of the hospital. They are patients who need attention as soon as possible. The opening of a new wing doesn't warrant that they be neglected."

Chad stood up and stretched his hand for PJ before they walked out of the office.

PJ flinched when Chad threw the jacket at the back seat of the car before he rolled his shirt.

"Get in," he commanded. She got into the car wondering where everyone had gone. Was he angry? She peeked under her lashes as he drove away from the hospital.

"My sis?"

"Your sister and the rest of the girls have been taken to the Grand hotel for lunch and pampering."

"And where are we going?" PJ asked as she realized he had taken a turn towards her home. Chad didn't answer but continued looking straight ahead. She wondered what was going on in that mind of his since he looked so determined.

Once they got to the house, her step mother must have heard the car because she came out of the house and her first question was about Edwina.

"Edwina is at the Grand hotel with the rest of the girls," Chad answered. "I believe I've a meeting with Mr. James."

Adele frowned but couldn't pass some snide comments on her careless step daughter, especially with the prince looking at her to lead the way. She nodded and walked ahead. What had PJ done this time around, she wondered.

A slight knock on the study before the door was opened. "Thank you, Mrs. James," Chad said.

"PJ can remain behind," he continued while the woman huffed and shut the door.

Mr. James was smiling at him yet curiously looking at his daughter who had remained behind.

"I have a complaint against your daughter," Chad began while PJ gasped and nearly fell in a faint. No way was he going to tell her father pertaining to an arrangement she had tried to make. Chad couldn't be that cruel as to give her old man a heart attack.

"I doubt my sweet Pea could ever disappoint. She might be stubborn like her mother but she always considers other people first before anything else," her father said with a chuckle and motioned for Chad to take a seat.

"Indeed," Chad said and settled down.

By the time the two men were done talking, her father had agreed to the prince that PJ would be his legal representative and easily available to him, as his manager.

"Wow, just like that without giving me a say on the matter," PJ said following behind the prince once the meeting with her dad was over.

"As a woman, do I even have a say in this." Chad shook his head and leaned in before he whispered in her ear. "That offer you made, I accept," he said then hungrily kissed her with the promise of what would happen with the two of them once they were alone. PJ was taken by surprise at first but as usual Chad managed to crumble those walls, she wanted to build around her heart with just his touch.

She clung to him from the onslaught, moaning while she pulled him closer and pressed onto his hard chest.

Chad shifted away, grinned then turned to open the door to his car. PJ's eyes widened while the prince smirked with that knowing look of having shocked her and rendered her speechless.

"See you bright and early Miss James," he said before he drove off.

Hell, what have I got myself into, was the thought that filtered into her mind before she stamped her feet, heaved a breath preparing herself from the onslaught of her step mother and walked back into the house?

Chapter 16

FOR the following months, PJ was seen in all the places where Chad went. She had become somewhat of a darling to the women since she had always strived to accommodate all, while others said a few unsavory remarks, casting aspersions over her relationship with the prince.

Chad, on the other hand, didn't seem to care at all, instead he accommodated her in public in the same manner he did to the girls he was meant to select his bride from. He would dance with them at functions and dance with PJ as well amidst her protests.

"People are looking," she would usually whisper below her breath while he looked sternly at her. "So, are you going to refuse to dance with me because of people?" Or brother, why even try to reason with him as he was bent on proving her decision wrong.

PJ slid the strawberry into the melted chocolate before chewing thoughtfully at it while she looked at yet another aspect that had to be dealt with, the prince's search for a bride. All the girls looked good on paper. She flipped the profiles. None of them appeared to be exerting any rights or doing something notable apart from attending functions.

What Chad needed was an equal, not a woman who would be there to just look pretty. Actually, what their kingdom needed were more women taking leadership roles. It was a long stretch but PJ hoped since Chad had been brought up in a different environment the way he thought was different from his forefathers who had kept a tight leash over their women.

Chad cleared his throat bringing PJ to the present. He was standing by the mirror failing to tie a knot on his necktie. Meghan had been good at doing that for him.

"Sonia might do," PJ said before she finished off with her strawberry and walked towards where he stood. She took charge of helping him with his tie before she helped him with the jacket.

"I thought you would suggest Edwina," Chad said while PJ rolled her eyes. Ever since she became Chad's manager Edwina had been making herself scarce. She wondered where she disappeared to since the mother always assumed she was with Chad.

"Edwina thinks you are ancient," PJ retorted while he grinned.

"The beauty of being a youth. Will Sonia hold my attention for long?"

"What do you mean? She is mature compared to the rest, her past records also show that she loves helping out as she is in a couple of charitable organizations and she can be discreet."

"My position needs someone who will be discreet, but apart from that I choose to be a faithful husband just like my father and great grandfather."

PJs hand stilled at the button as it slightly trembled.

"Oh," she said before Chad drew her close and passionately kissed her. She hadn't thought their arrangement would end and knowing that Chad would put an end to it, hurt like hell.

She suddenly felt like ordering a bottle of wine and getting drunk to forget about her woes.

"I will see you in the evening," Chad said and kissed her again as she clung to him for comfort. "Tonight," he whispered before he winked and walked out of the hotel room they had reserved for their stay while they were in the northern region of the kingdom.

• • ⌘ • •

"WHAT IS HAPPENING," Chad asked Morgan, his head of security and friend once he got back from his meeting. It was evening and he had failed to meet with the leader of the people who were said to be planning an insurgency in the kingdom.

His father had ordered him to investigate on a low key as he suspected some of his advisors of being shady. The King no longer trusted some of them and felt a lot was brewing beneath his nose which he wasn't aware of.

"I don't know what I am looking for here, is she working with any terrorist organization?"

Chad chuckled and looked at the screen.

"She has been in bed ever since you left. She did go out for a bit and came back with food and wine. Surprisingly she didn't touch the wine but was singing to Toni Braxton like a drunk person."

Chad laughed so PJ did care after all over their arrangement ending.

"How did the meeting go?" Morgan asked.

"As to be expected," he answered before he unloosened his tie.

"Any dinner parties being attended tonight so the security is on standby?"

"No, we are definitely staying in," Chad answered before he hit Morgan on the back and left. Morgan laughed wondering why Chad wasn't marrying PJ.

PJ didn't drink the wine, could she be, Chad wondered but shook his head. Drastic problems called for drastic solutions. He had changed the woman's birth control pills with some vitamin supplements in the hopes that if she got pregnant, she would stop this nonsense of him having a wife and mistress.

In the two months they had been together, he let her believe that he had accepted her choice to be his mistress. He knew that no one would come close to being like her. So why suffer through the process of getting to know someone else. That's why he decided to keep her by his side as they would get to know each other better and she realized how good they could be together.

"Chad," PJ rose from bed when he walked into the room. She had showered and looked fresh in her black lacy negligee.

She smelt good; he thought as she hungrily kissed him and removed his jacket. He had felt tired and frustrated as things appeared not to be going his way, but being met by such a lovely picture everyday put him in the mood for more.

"You surely don't wait for the man to take the lead," Chad remarked as PJ pushed him to the wall.

"You should give me the chance to climb the tree woman and pluck the fruit." PJ giggled before she removed the belt of his trousers, knelt on the floor and did something with her mouth that had Chad groaning loudly and hoping they would not be chased away from the hotel.

PJ ran her hand on Chad's face while he slept. What a mess she had made of their lives. She should have not taken Tony's words to heart and rejected Chad's proposal.

Now he wasn't even asking but rather had settled to the idea of her being his mistress. She touched her stomach. It was now official, she was pregnant. After he left for the meeting, she went out and ordered food before evading the security that was always at hand and bought a pregnancy kit that she hid from their view.

She had expected to see one single line but apparently her body had decided it was time to conceive despite the birth control she was on. She has always been careful when it came to that, not wanting to bring a child into her messed up life. Why!! She almost wailed.

She gasped when Chad pulled her close to his warm body and ran his hand on her tummy while he nuzzled her neck. A quiver ran down her spine and the butterflies started their fluttering as usual when he touched her.

"Morning baby," he whispered in his deep rumble of a voice while she giggled when she was turned over and kissed.

Yesterday had been phenomenal with Chad. Every time she coupled with him, it always felt different. She showered again this time with him as they made slow passionate love before they had dinner and cuddled in bed afterwards.

"Any plans for today?" PJ asked.

"You can take the much-needed day off. I have things to look into so I will be out." She huffed at that, "What is really going on. Even yesterday you were being secretive."

"Nothing that concerns this pretty head of yours," Chad answered and tweaked her nose. She leaned in for the kiss and whispered afterwards, "I love you." The damned man groaned and yelped when she pinched him. "I just said I love you."

"I heard you loud and clear," he said and rose from the bed. She missed his warm body on her side. "Well, the least you can do if a lady told you they love you is to say you love them back."

Chad grabbed the robe on the bed. "No way, woman," he dodged the pillow that she threw his way. "You still have to control that violent streak, maybe then I might consider loving you back," he said with a wink before he walked toward the adjoining bathroom. PJ sighed and slumped her head back on the pillow. It was time she visited the library and community where her mother had started a foundation to help educate the girl child. Lately some shipments had gone missing and she wanted to get to the bottom of why it was happening.

• • ❧ • •

"PJ THANK YOU AGAIN for the books," Mrs. Dickens the librarian said and settled next to her before handing her the mug of coffee.

"It's always a pleasure," PJ said, then took a sip of the coffee and asked, "Are there any leads pertaining to the missing boxes?"

Mrs. Dickens shook her head and answered "Nothing," with a frown on her face. "Are you sure that the number of boxes we received is different from the one you signed off on? These papers right here show that what we received is what was sent."

"Pretty sure," PJ said. "And this has been going on for quite some time. Mother never realized because her condition had worsened whilst she insisted on working and when I took over, I didn't realize what was happening fast enough."

Mrs. Dickens touched her face on that note, "You are so like your mother, beautiful inside and out. I miss her."

PJ removed her hand and cradled it instead. "So do I," she whispered.

"I can't believe that she continued working, despite the pain she must have felt over the chemo."

PJ smiled at the thought of her mother, "She always told me that seeing a smile from just one child she managed to help, or catching them laughing out of joy made the pain go away. Did you know she used to beg me to wheel her to the children's ward just to see their joyful expressions at receiving the toys she would have sent?"

"That's your mother, our good Samaritan," Mrs. Dickens said with a chuckle.

"Speaking about good Samaritans, there is one meant to come in today with more supplies."

"Are you talking about the good Samaritan who was able to think about providing sanitary wear to the teen girls?"

"Yes, the very one."

"I wonder why I never thought about that though, it still bothers me, it really does," PJ said as she rubbed her chin while Mrs. Dickens laughed. Who wouldn't be bothered at all if they found out that a man was the one behind thinking about girls' hygiene and menstrual cycles instead of women?

"You have too many things on your mind, don't beat yourself over that, the community appreciates what the Ellen foundation does, the clothes, tuition for the girls, library full of books and food hampers."

A sound of a truck was heard outside that had the old woman scrambling to her feet like a spry teen.

"That must be him. He happens to still be single too and might be your type. Handsome, tall but I should warn you, not mysterious. He is an open book, a man who would love and cherish you for the rest of your life," she stated with a wink while PJ giggled at her sudden burst of energy. And to think the old woman had been whining to her about aching bones.

PJ decided to stall the meeting further with the mystery man. Mrs. Dickens wasn't aware that she already had that kind of man already in her life.

She worked at restocking the books while she kept an eye on the boxes that were being moved to the storeroom by the workers. The benefactor surely knew how to be generous, seeing the boxes were still coming in.

Finally, she heard Mrs. Dickens' voice and picked out the last load of books in the box.

"PJ I would like you to meet an old friend."

PJ straightened up with a smile that froze before it widened. "Chad," she greeted while the old woman swatted her arm. "The prince mind you."

Chad grinned, "Nice to see you again Miss Peggy James."

"You know each other," Mrs. Dickens asked, confused at the same time looking at both of them.

That wink boded on worse than good, PJ thought and rushed to Chad when he opened his mouth to speak. She clamped it with her hand while Mrs. Dickens gasped in shock.

"I am his legal advisor," she said and pulled her hand away when Chad nipped at it.

"Can't you see Mrs. Dickens is about to have a heart attack babe over you being too familiar with the prince."

"So, you are the woman that everyone has been talking about, in that the prince has a female advisor," the old woman said and looked disapprovingly at PJ.

PJ groaned, "Blame it on him and dad. I didn't have a choice over becoming his advisor."

Mrs. Dickens chuckled and pulled her ear while she yelped. "It is a good thing; everyone is actually smitten and admires the prince with what has been accomplished ever since he took you on board."

"Seriously?" PJ asked and managed to remove her ear from the old woman's grasp. "I thought you would be opposed, seeing that some of the papers didn't have anything good to say but rather pointed out that I might be having an affair with Chad."

"I am happy with the state affairs, what you do with your private lives is none of my business."

Wow, PJ almost shouted and threw her arms around the old woman. If her granny could act in the same manner then she had the chance of fixing things with Chad after all. Mrs. Dickens was best friends with her granny, so wouldn't her granny tell her that her private life was hers like her friend had done. She looked at Chad who was chatting with the old woman.

Chad looked up to her as if sensing her staring at him. He smiled and asked, "Shall we go."

"Are you not leaving with the other men and Mrs. Dickens might still need me to help around?"

He slid his hands into his pockets. "I took a peek into your schedule while you were taking a shower and noticed you intend to pay a visit to your granny, that's the reason why I came here, and of course to see my beautiful woman," he finished with a wink at Mrs. Dickens who laughed in return at his antics.

Ok, this is the part when she wished the ground would open up and swallow her. The old woman didn't seem to notice the blunder but called Chad a flatterer. "We are done; you can take her along with you." She smiled and hugged PJ before hugging Chad. Once they reached her car, PJ asked, "Did you really have to point out that I was taking a shower when you looked at my diary."

"Were you not?" Chad took the keys from her and got into the driver's seat while she huffed and went to the passenger side.

"She might think we are," she paused, "as the articles suggest," she lamely finished.

"Are we not?" Chad raised a brow while she wrung her arms helplessly.

"I give up," she said and slumped on the seat then crossed her arms over her breast. They were silent as Chad drove while PJ imagined the worst reaction from her granny.

"Speak," Chad commanded and had her clutching on her seat belt because he had startled her. How was she going to wiggle herself out of this one? She cleared her throat, "Are you done with your business for today. I don't want you leaving your work half done so you can take me to my granny's place."

"Is that the reason why you failed to mention it in the morning?"

PJ wrung her hands. "Well, my granny is not like Mrs. Dickens. She is old fashioned Chad and if she read those other articles, she might not be as welcoming as you think."

He stopped the car and got out.

"Baby what are you doing?"

"Letting you visit her alone is what I am doing," Chad replied after PJ followed him out of the car. He looked back to where they had come from while PJ almost drooled at the blue jeans and how they snuggly hugged his tall frame. He had changed from his suit before he went to the library. He flagged a car that was coming their way. The car started slowing down while PJ clutched at his arm to stop him.

She hated parting with him on angry terms. Just like any normal couple they did fight, a lot actually but it always ended in them making up after. She could be stubborn and she realized that her man could be hot headed as well. Just look at the way he just stopped the car and started flagging another, without waiting for her to fully explain. Huh!

"Hello handsome, where to," the lady in the car, rolled her window and smiled at Chad while PJ wished to slug her. Did such women exist in their kingdom? Too forward indeed. With Chad in his casuals, the woman wouldn't even recognize him as the prince.

"You can go, he is with me," she spoke and literally huffed when the lady grinned at Chad not paying attention to her.

"You heard the lady," Chad said with a regretful half grin on his face that had PJ snorting. He really was milking the moment. The lady reached out to her purse on the side. "If it doesn't work out, call me," she said, handing him her card, winking at him before driving off.

"I guess I have still got it," Chad said with a grin, jiggled his broad chest and showed his muscles, while PJ stamped her feet in frustration and got into the car.

Once in the car Chad turned to her and took her hand, "I am not trying to put you in a tight spot, really. I am okay if you went on your own."

"And watch you date another woman as revenge," she snorted while Chad chuckled and tilted her chin. "Jealous."

He sighed. "PJ you are the only woman I am crazy about. Like I said, I am not angry. So can I go?"

PJ held his hand. "It's fine, we can go together. I have to warn you though the old woman is sharp. When she found out about dad's affair, she helped mom leave with me for the states and got estranged from her only son. She might not give credence to what the articles say, but one look at us will tell her everything. Dad called her a witch once since she was always a step ahead."

Chad chuckled. "I can't wait to meet her."

PJ pulled at the seat belt before muttering, "Don't say I didn't warn you."

Chapter 17

IT wasn't what she expected when her granny opened the door. Actually, PJ was reeling from the shock as her granny welcomed them into her lovely home while Chad winked at her bewildered face. Clever Chad, he had slipped a ring on her finger and assured her that it will be fine and she shouldn't think much about it.

He wanted her granny to like him too, so being a traditional person there's only one thing that could silence her, the ring and that worked like a charm.

The snide comments that her granny would pull out from the top of her head never came. PJ watched her from beneath her lashes after dinner while they were in the living room as the old girl seemed to be quite enjoying Chad's company.

The diamond ring weighed heavily on her finger and at having to pretend in front of her granny. With a baby on the way, she really needed that proposal after all.

When it was time for them to retire to bed the old curmudgeon announced, "My prince, the guest room has been prepared for you. PJ you will sleep in my room tonight." PJ should have realized that the old girl as usual had seen more than she was letting on.

"Granny I wouldn't want to take away your beauty sleep, there are plenty of rooms..."

"No, you sleep in my room," her grandmother firmly said before she stood up, said goodnight to Chad and glided from the living room like a queen. At seventy her granny's posture still remained perfect and she didn't wiggle or shuffle like the other old women but her slender figure remained ramrod straight. PJ could almost imagine what a looker she had been in her younger days, and she had the photos to prove that too.

"Great, I can't sneak into your room after all," PJ huffed while Chad grinned and rubbed her arms once her granny left the room.

"It's just for tonight."

"Well, I am now used to sleeping with you."

Chad chuckled at her petulant expression.

"Believe me baby, I want you in the same manner," he said, tilting her chin up.

"You should have commanded her to put us in one room since we are now engaged."

Chad stared at her for a while as she squirmed a bit under his gaze before he commented, "Lately you are becoming too emotional, are you sure you are fine. Besides, the ring was for you not to get into trouble. Are you not content with your little arrangement?"

PJ huffed and stamped her feet before she walked away.

Chad chuckled and rushed to her then pulled her into his arms and kissed her deeply.

"Good night," he said after they drew apart then he pushed her to her Granny's room, before she could recover.

She had almost blurted out that she wasn't content, but she knew Chad. He would want to know why her sudden change of heart.

"Right, are you done with acting like a common whore so we get this test over with," her granny asked once she got into her room.

Apparently, her best behavior had been for Chad only. Her granny looked at her disapprovingly while PJ gulped down a few breaths and walked further into the room.

"Test?" she tentatively asked in the hope that it wasn't what she was thinking.

"Get a move on I don't have the whole night for this, lie down so we see what you have been up to. As the prince's bride you will undergo this and much more."

"About that granny, believe me it's quite a long story."

Her granny crossed her arms over her breast and looked broodingly at her.

I will tell her quickly, PJ thought, *but where to start from?* Chad said that didn't apply to them but seeing her granny's stern face told her otherwise.

PJ lowered her eyes to the carpeted floor and brushed on her jeans as her hands suddenly felt clammy.

Jeez, didn't these people believe in one's sexual life being private and not to be paraded. She gulped down a few breaths, thinking back when her mother spoke about her first time, how they retrieved the white sheet and showed the elders that she had been a virgin.

Here goes nothing.

"I can't participate in that test because I'm not a virgin." There she had spoken it out, loud and clearly at the same time feeling a bit humiliated. Her granny could as well hurl a few insults at her, like Tony had done; glossing over the fact that she would never be with Chad since she wasn't suitable. She had spurned the laws and traditions even going against her roots.

A long silence followed that had PJ looking up and was in time to see her granny's ashen face before she slumped down on the arm chair. PJ rushed to her in alarm, knelt down and clasped her hands. "Granny!" she hollered.

"Chad knows about this and he understands." Her granny snatched her hands from her before hitting her hard on the back with the sandal she had retrieved from her foot.

PJ squealed and tried to escape the old woman who had grabbed her with the other hand and was still hitting her.

"Granny I am an adult," she cried and tried to wiggle herself from the firm grasp. She nearly shouted; this is abuse but swallowed her pride of having to sound like a teen instead of the adult she professed to be.

The old girl snorted. "Does he know you are breeding too?" Another whack on the back and head followed. Her granny must have known the instant she saw her, those sharp eyes never missed anything.

"Tell me foolish girl, is it his or that good for nothing Tony."

PJ shook her head. "It's his." Her grandmother heaved a sigh of relief, sat back on the chair and threw the sandal away.

PJ scurried away from her. Seriously at twenty-four she was still being subjected to such treatment.

"At least for once you thought with your head. I don't know what it is with you kids of nowadays, treating sex like you are riding a bicycle. Throwing away the values instilled in you to receive a cheap thrill of three seconds maybe even less."

"Grandma," PJ huffed. Seeing her granny had recovered from her shock, her mouth quivered at the edges. "Since there is nothing to lose, can I go to him?"

Her granny incredulously looked at her and chuckled, "Very shameless indeed, not under my roof little missy, I am not that modern in my thinking. No more sleeping with the prince until you are married, and I will make sure of that," her grandma threatened before she stood up from the chair.

PJ threw her arms around her at the sight of her smile. "Thank you grandma, I thought you would be disappointed that's why I intended to come alone and inform you, except Chad..." she flared her arms. It's not like he had insisted, she had felt bad when he was about to go back and let her continue with her journey.

Her granny cradled her face. "I am disappointed but happy that he will do right by you."

Her grandma reached for the hand with the ring, "But PJ," she sadly said and shook her head. "I wonder if the elders will be this lenient like I have been. The queen that they expect is one who adheres to their way of life. I guess your mom's quest for your freedom also took that away," she grimaced before letting go of her hand and getting into bed.

PJ silently took the night shirt on that damper note and removed her clothes before she got ready for bed. Her granny was already snoring by the time she got into bed. PJ played over her last statement. How would the elders react to her falling pregnant before she was married even if that child happened to be the prince's?

For the first time she felt dread. Maybe she should never have suggested being Chad's mistress. She gritted her teeth and hit the pillow before lying down and falling into a fitful sleep.

The next day she woke up, she felt tired as she had tossed and turned during the night. And what was Chad doing, snoring away in the guest room. This was all his fault, he should have said, *baby let's wait for marriage.*

As if she would have followed that advice if given the chance. Her grandmother was content in not pulling strings or giving a solution to all this mess.

Why was she taking out her anger on them anyways, these were the decisions she had made? She recalled back to when Chad asked her if she was sure about this. Well, she wasn't thinking straight then. She was fighting a demon from the past, Tony who had called her a log in bed and she wanted it to be different with Chad.

God this was such a mess. What if she left for the States gave birth and came back? Or she proposed to Chad and got married without the fuss.

In my dreams, she loudly spoke and yanked the covers from her body before walking to the bathroom and getting ready to face her granny and finally tell Chad that she had been careless.

• • ✿ • •

AS PJ LEFT FOR THE study after her breakfast, having ordered the maid to prepare a basket of goodies, she smiled. She tossed the car keys into the air and chuckled when she caught them. It is said that the way to a man's heart is through his stomach, so she had planned out a picnic before she broke the news to Chad. Maybe he would not think her careless once she fed him at her favorite spot near the pond. He would be fine with it and he was more than ready to become a dad.

Tony's image drifted into her mind of a memory never forgotten, but always at the back of her mind. He told her that he didn't want any kids and would leave if she ever made that mistake. Chad was different right. Besides thirty years was actually a good age to start a family. By the time Chad was in his early fifties, their son would be done with college.

Who was she kidding here? She was totally freaking out. If Chad had wanted a child out of wedlock, he would have had a bunch with Cherise.

Stupid, stupid girl, she thought as her feet slowed down, no longer looking forward to the picnic.

She frowned as she came closer to the study and she could hear her granny's raised voice and Chad's curt retorts.

What was going on, she wondered and increased her pace. Chad came out of the study and didn't glance her way but walked out.

PJ got into the study. Her granny was settled on the chair, with a smirk on her face.

"Granny what did you tell Chad, I know you are disappointed in the both of us but you have no right."

The old woman snorted. "Not everything revolves around you." PJ heard the front door slam shut and looked at the smug woman before she rushed after Chad.

"Just go back into the house PJ," Chad curtly said once she caught up with him. He wasn't in the mood to deal with another James woman who thought she was smart and could take things into her own hands.

"What happened?"

"Nothing." Chad looked at her before saying firmly, "Give me your car key."

"I will do no such thing until you tell me what's going on."

Chad groaned, "I just want to attend to something before we leave."

"Does that something have a name?"

"The key," Chad stretched out his hand. She hid her hand behind her back.

"PJ stop acting like a child."

"News flash Prince Chadwick, I have a right to refuse with my keys."

He walked towards her while she tried to escape. Grabbing her before she made a dash for it, Chad mumbled, "I wonder why you have to resist, knowing I can get what I want from you by doing just this." She gasped as he gently kissed her, before deepening the kiss and her body quivered to the sensation as usual.

Chad pried the key from her hand since she had forgotten about what she had been trying to hide and was relieved of not having something in her hand to stop her from running her hands on his neck and his hair. Chad pulled away when she wanted more and grinned at her before he got into the car. PJ stamped her feet and opened the passenger door. No way was he going alone.

"You might have managed to get the key but I am sticking to you like glue."

He shook his head. "Suit yourself," he muttered before he slid the key into the ignition.

An hour later PJ was regretting having followed Chad. They had stopped some thirty minutes ago at a deserted spot and continued to trek since the road wasn't wide enough for cars. She wasn't much of a hiking kind of girl, while her prince charming was content to lead her, the Lord only knew where.

She had contemplated on pretending to have a sprained ankle, but she and Chad had dressed comfortably and for such a walk hence she knew that lie would not hold water.

Maybe if she had worn heels with her short dress, she would have pulled it off. But instead, she had worn hiking boots, her short flowery dress and a denim jacket, since she had to trek a short distance too in order to get to her favorite pond for their picnic.

Chad claimed she could be a drama queen so for once she wanted to be on her best behavior, buttering him up for the news of course.

Her attention got drawn to his tall form as the black polo t-shirt showed off his muscles. She longed to have been that t-shirt wrapped around his body. The t-shirt must have been celebrating, being tautly stretched on that body and the jeans...her mind went numb.

Come to think of it, her granny wasn't anywhere near to stop her from her wicked thoughts. Pulling on the formula she knew would not work, she yelped, "Ouch," as Chad quickly turned around more attuned to her distress than anyone could be.

"Baby," he looked at her with concern and for a second, she felt guilty.

"I think I stepped on my foot the wrong way. It hurts."

Chad swiftly carried her to a huge boulder that he noticed on the side of the path.

"Where does it hurt," he asked as he removed her boot and sock from the supposedly hurt foot. She pointed at the non-existent aching spot. Chad massaged her ankle and she nearly groaned.

"For a person with a hurt ankle, you surely know how to move your foot around."

PJ opened her eyes and was in time to see an amused expression on his face. She had been moaning with her eyes shut from his tender touch while his hand had trailed from her ankle up her leg to her thighs, apparently having the same idea of fun as she did.

"You can't fault a girl for trying," she giggled while Chad put her sock on and then her boot.

"You forget they might be snakes, wild animals and creatures lurking around."

"Who knew you were so picky," she sneered as he helped her stand. Seriously is that what he could say. She looked around wondering if her grandmother was around, seeing the old girl had informed her that she would not be able to sleep with the prince until they were married.

"I will make it up to you. But not here, now we have to move fast. I am still debating on whether it was a good idea to bring you along in the first place."

She huffed. "These days you are acting all uppity Prince Chadwick Johnson. Don't act like you don't like running your hands on my leg, your hand even trailed to my thigh."

Chad chuckled at his emotional woman. It was official, she definitely was pregnant. When she had yelped, he had feared it was the baby and was relieved when she pointed to the foot. His ears were still ringing from the peals of reprimands he had received from her granny as she had given him an ultimatum in rectifying his mistake. The old woman just didn't get it that her granddaughter was the stubborn one in all this.

He humored PJ by cradling her face and slanting her head so he could have better access to those sweet lips, squashing away the protests. PJ wound her arms around his neck and pressed herself firmly against his chest while Chad's hands trailed at the back then her hips before he pulled her closer, making her aware of how hard he was for her. "Is this what you want," Chad growled as he swiftly picked her and had her legs straddling him on his waist.

"Yeah baby," PJ squealed while he chuckled.

"You are a hussy you know that. My first impression was right after all."

PJ giggled, not at all offended. She was a hussy with him because he loved her. That was one thought that boosted her confidence. Chad loved her.

"Stop talking and kiss me," she whispered before lowering her head and receiving the kiss she always anticipated. Chad could make love to her mouth with his full strong lips as he had a way of drawing out all her inhibitions by just kissing her senseless. PJ moaned as their tongues stroked and her body quivered at the sensation.

PJ pulled away nearly giggling when she felt the bark of a tree on her back. Not ideal after all, she thought. She could be spontaneous but in bed. Chad cleared his throat and shifted, becoming aware of his surroundings, for a second there he had nearly got carried away.

"Now with that out of the way, can we proceed?" Chad asked and slid his fingers into hers before they started walking.

"By the way, where are we going?"

Chad motioned for her to keep quiet and stood still.

PJ froze when one man emerged holding a rifle in his hand. She yelped. Her eyes further widened as men with rifles suddenly surrounded them. They were dressed in dark clothes and looked menacing.

"Chad we should get out of here," PJ whispered, afraid of what would happen. All thoughts of seducing her man suddenly fled to be replaced by an image of being murdered in broad daylight but tortured first before that happened.

She should have attentively listened to her father who was more aware of the things happening in the kingdom, since he had mentioned something about terrorists living in the wilderness and being a menace.

A man emerged from the crew and asked, "Who are you and what do you want?" The proper answer to such a question would have been a lie as they cited that they were lost and they would leave if the menacing men pointed the way. But her prince charming of course had none of that in his mind.

"Prince Chadwick at your service," Chad responded proudly to PJs horror. Bummer.

She hadn't expected him to say that. By the way the men were now looking at him with interest as if he had served himself up as their meal ticket.

Mama I guess I will see you sooner than anticipated, PJ thought. The man who had addressed Chad roared in laughter before saying, "there isn't a prince in these woods apart from me."

He looked at PJ as she shivered. Chad pulled her possessively to his side and there was a threat in his eyes that made the man slightly lower his eyes.

"Although I have heard of another prince, he is a great fighter and you sir don't look like one."

"Why don't you put me to the test and we see?" Chad replied calmly.

"Come along," the man motioned as Chad nodded and made PJ walk in front of him. She nearly huffed yet at the same time felt comforted that he was behind her after having witnessed the men leer and wink at her.

What had she gotten herself into? She should have listened to him when he told her to go back into the house. When has she ever listened to him though? He wanted to marry her and she turned him down flatly and decided to be his mistress instead. He guessed she was pregnant and she was so confident with her birth control pills, and now, this.

They came to a clearing and PJ gasped at noticing the crudely built huts and people coming from them. A village with men and women of all ages. She spotted some kids chasing each other and playing. They were led further and PJ nearly protested when they came to a clearing again, this time with bloody people pummeling each other with bare fists.

It took her a second to realize that Chad would be fighting when he removed his shirt and introductions were yelled out. A crowd was beginning to gather with curious expressions at the two strangers.

PJ uncomfortably smiled at some girls who were intensely looking at her. It's not like she was any different from them, apart from the fact that they had experienced the hardships of life while she had been brought up in luxury. Their skin tones were of a darker shade while for the first time she felt alien.

The girls smiled in return, putting her at ease. *Not an alien after all,* she muttered under her breath before looking to where Chad was.

A giant of a man appeared, the village champion that had PJ almost falling in a faint.

Chad walked to her and kissed her hard. "If I don't make it, run like hell," he whispered before he got into the ring made by people and PJ almost yelled at him for saying that.

She didn't want to look but still stared in fascination as the opponents sized each other up. Though Chad, compared to the champion, was lighter in built, it proved to be to his advantage as the man was slower. PJ yelled, "Yeah baby," when Chad managed to punch the man and avoided getting punched in return.

She was fascinated by his movements, how his skin glistened and the bulge of his muscles as they flexed. This is getting out of hand, she muttered under her breath at noticing that she had joined the crowd in hollering at the top of their lungs, urging the fighters on.

She screamed when Chad fell with a dull thud on the ground before he woke up and staggered. She couldn't watch this. She turned aside at the sight of blood coming from his nose suddenly feeling stifled. Seeing leering faces as they started blurring before her, PJ fell in a faint.

The village champion had nearly got him, Chad thought as he rubbed his nose. Seeing the blood, he grinned. It had been long and he was quite enjoying the adrenaline rush.

He looked to where PJ had been standing expecting to hear her holler like she had been doing at the top of her lungs.

A few gasps were heard when he had kissed her and at her endearment of baby but she didn't notice and continued urging him on. Of course, he had been joking about her having to escape if he didn't make it.

He caught sight of her falling in a faint. The champion got that opportunity to place another facer that made him see double and his ears ring. *Enough,* Chad growled, ducked before he got hit again and with one hard fist to his face had the champion in a daze before he fell on the ground.

Chad did not wait to hear what the announcer was saying as he rushed to PJ. Women, he thought as the leader of the crew, came to where he stood with his woman in his arms. "Prince Chadwick, we welcome you to our village," Gerard, his childhood friend, said and finally smiled at him.

"I guess the foreign land didn't make you soft. We are ready for the talk, thank you for agreeing to meet with us," he continued and motioned for Chad to follow.

Chapter 18

PJ slowly opened her eyes to an unfamiliar room and sat up. The lady waiting on her rushed to her and gave her water. She was feeling thirsty hence took it and gulped it down. It tasted of smoke and charcoal as she opened her eyes wide before the events of what had happened sifted into her mind.

"Is Chad alive," she whispered in fear while the woman laughed.

"The prince is alive and well. He knocked our champion out with just one knock to his face."

"Are you sure?"

The lady giggled at seeing the disbelief in her face, "Yes. The prince is a good fighter and everyone knows that about him. He knocked the champion out quickly because he was in a rush to come to you. Usually, he enjoys the fight and drags it on."

PJ blushed at that fact. So, Chad knew these people after all and he failed to mention that to her but rather let her believe that he would die in the fight. Clearing her throat, she looked around the hut. "What is this place?"

"It's a temporary settlement that we managed to build after we lost our homes," the lady answered before PJ asked further and got the answers she needed.

Chad entered the hut after supper and long talk with his friend and the elders. He found a smiling PJ not at all the scared woman he had witnessed before and had him rush the match so he could go to her.

She swung her legs from the bed before she rushed into his arms. "I wish you could do this more often," he said while she looked up at him and touched his tender nose.

"Are you going to be, okay?"

He shrugged, "it's nothing. I will survive."

"How did your meeting go? I gather this is the reason why you came here?" Chad frowned. He looked disturbed before he replied, "Not good, especially after seeing the pathetic condition that people I know have been subjected to."

He went on to tell her about his friend and why he had made himself a leader to these people. "I think it's time I had a chat with my dad's advisory committee because I am trying to understand how they could overlook the fact that they left people destitute after giving the Eastlea Investment company rights to mine on the land. The situation is bad as you can see." He looked around the hut they were in. "They have no clean running water, no medical facility or schools to develop their children. The company hasn't done anything it promised apart from polluting the land with its mining activity without improving the plight of the local people. Sturdy homes PJ were destroyed in the quest of development and what do the elders say about that. That they are terrorists lurking around and bringing terror to the nearby villages. You also saw how we had to walk from the main road to here."

PJ nodded since Dorothy; her new friend had filled her in on everything pertaining to the settlement. "Is that what granny was telling you in the morning?"

Chad chuckled, "Yes, it is sweet Pea, what did you think?" Her grandmother had more than laid it thick before giving the letter from Gerard.

"Well, I thought," PJ gulped down a few breaths and mumbled "never mind." She had thought the old woman had told Chad about the pregnancy.

"Come let me show you something," Chad pulled her towards the door. As they walked past each hut, PJs heart nearly tore at the dire situation. Chad pulled her into a bigger hut that looked much better and well maintained than the rest. She gasped once they were inside.

"So, this is where my books have been disappearing to," she remarked, taking in the shelves with books.

"They didn't steal the books." Chad was saying when PJ waved her hand. "I know granny must be the one who had made adjustments on the order. Seeing how she connected you with these people." She looked around on the corner and saw a space with medication, well stocked and off course the boxes of sanitary wear. Mrs. Dickens must have known all this, that's why she was delaying and would change the subject over involving authorities.

Chad smiled at that. "Don't be too hard on your granny. In my books she is a saint not a witch like your father said. I now see what you meant by her being sharp. Dad had sent me to look into an insurgence that was brewing. He gave me a heads up since I knew the leader, as it turns out; Gerard came here to help his parents once he found out about the displacement. When he tried to use the proper channels to speak pertaining to the plight, no door was being opened, apparently getting to speak to the King has become harder than before." Chad rubbed his hair in frustration. "The King is not aware of what is happening around him but suspects that something is brewing. He hasn't received any emails, petitions and pleas that have been made so far from the villages with the same problems of displacement."

"I get the building of temporary shelters and all. What about the rifles? In order to get those, one needs a financial backing of some sort," PJ asked with a frown. "Maybe the elders were right and these were terrorists."

Chad laughed and kissed those cute lips. "Hunting rifles, I guess they scared you." He cradled that beautiful face and frowned. "If fighting for your rights makes one a terrorist, then they are that. They are willing to fight for the land if they are to be displaced again from here, as it is; the minister of land was quick to point out that they had illegally settled here." Chad scoffed. "I wonder where they expect them to go since they didn't provide them with an alternative after the displacement. PJ these are just common folks who want to fight for the injustice done to them. Gerard saw an article in that I was back but somehow was barred from meeting me. I wasn't aware about the extra security. Then when he saw the one about you being my manager and added two and two together from your surname. That's how he asked your granny for help in the hopes she could use you to get to me. Apparently, she has been working alongside them and helping where needed."

PJ nodded, understanding a bit why the old woman had been persisting over her visiting her at her country home instead of the town house where she usually stays. She huffed. Had her granny suspected that Chad would want to accompany her?

"I wish you could be more like her," Chad was saying, "or I would have to marry the old woman on the spot than stick with you my emotional lady who swoons at the sight of blood."

PJ huffed and pinched Chad for saying that. "Baby," Chad said and cradled her face again before kissing her deeply. After they had pulled away, he whispered. "Now I need you to do something for me."

"You can't be serious," PJ said after Chad was done talking.

"It's not enough my being here, I need to stay on a bit longer and also visit the mines. They are also other settlements like this one, but whilst I do so, I need you to convey all my messages to the king. Your dad will assist you in the area of meeting with the King and no one would think it amiss since you are always seen with me."

She finally nodded. He handed her the camera, it appears her knight had been at work, taking pics of the village and its inhabitants. He had taken a picture of the nearest river, where the villagers got their water. A few dead fish were floating on it. Her mouth suddenly went dry at the thought of drinking that water and she nearly buffed.

"Relax, there is a small canal that they use to fetch their drinking water and boil it." That explained the smoke she had tasted in the water.

"What if the king shouts, off with her head, how could she enter the courts of judgment before he even hears me out" she asked instead.

"My dad is not like that. I promise you will be safe."

"If I die, I will haunt you for the rest of your life," she threatened.

"He knows the love I have for you, nothing will happen, which brings me to this," he touched her hand. "I love you PJ and this is the last time."

"Yes,"

"I will ask you to marry me. What did you say?" Chad asked, confused since she had agreed before he finished his well-planned out proposal.

PJ giggled, "I said yes."

He crossed his arms, "Why the sudden change and quick reply. Are you expecting?"

PJ stamped her feet, "The witch, I knew she told you."

Chad pulled her back into his arms. "I already knew. I have noticed the mood swings from a mile away, besides," he shrugged his broad shoulders, "I might have substituted your birth control pills with my vitamins. Have you ever noticed how those damn tablets look the same?"

"You what!!" PJ screeched after pulling away from him while Chad shut his ears and had the audacity to grin at her. All the while she had thought it was her fault and he might not be ready to be a dad.

"I can't believe you did that," she yelled at the same time feeling relieved that she had been freaking out over nothing.

"Believe me; I could stoop even further than this just to get you."

She was still contemplating on how to respond to that and settled to laughing at the contrite expression he managed to pull on.

She went back into his strong arms.

"Ouch, ouch," Chad yelped as PJ pinched his ear. A laugh was heard near the door.

"After you are done fighting like siblings, please do join us outside," Gerard said before he left the lovebirds.

PJ and Chad walked out of the library. She clutched his arm and looked up to the sky, marveling at the stars and bright moon. How she had missed seeing this view.

They followed the path where everyone appeared to be headed to. She almost squealed when she noticed a bonfire and everyone settling wherever. Chad was offered a seat and pulled PJ onto his lap. She snuggled into his strong sturdy arms and looked on to the wide-open space in the middle.

A hushed silence fell. Some masked men and women emerged from the people and the story telling began. PJ watched in fascination at the dance and the characters, the slow tempo of drums playing in the background, the actors' movements as the story unfolded. Chad squeezed her hand as she suddenly felt she was finally home with her own people.

Chapter 19

"PJ help..." her young sister weakly spoke over the phone as PJ cleared the cobwebs in her head, waking up from her deep slumber. She had reluctantly answered the phone and grumbled a bit when it rang.

As Chad had said the day she left him in the village, the King was more than willing to listen to what she had to say.

She had gone to the palace with her father as advised. In the two days she was home and she hadn't seen Edwina or her step mother for that matter.

"Edwina, where are you?" PJ asked, battling the tiredness that had settled over her body.

"The City hospital, private wing."

"What are you..." she never got to finish because the next moment she heard a scream and something crushing on the floor.

"Edwina, Edwina!" she yelled but no one answered except for the fading sound of footsteps and of Edwina's screams before it suddenly became quiet. PJ got up from bed and rushed to the bathroom to brush her teeth.

She tried calling her step mother and her calls kept on going to her voicemail instead. She couldn't go knocking on her dad's bedroom door as she feared worrying him. Her father had a heart condition hence she might worry him unnecessarily and do more damage than good.

Maybe it was nothing and Edwina was just playing a prank on her.

After she was done with washing her face and brushing her teeth, she rushed to the wardrobe where she pulled out some clean sweat pants and t-shirt before she ran to Edwina's room hoping it was a prank call after all, despite the number being of the Hospital.

Edwina wasn't there and her bed was still made up, showing that she hadn't slept at home. Edwina usually left her bed unmade and would easily point out to PJ once she complained about it, on what was the use of having workers if she did their work for them.

It was still the early hours of the morning, hence the household was beginning to stir and only a few servants were up, so PJ was able to rush out using the back entrance without encountering any of them on the way.

By the time she got to the hospital, she was almost in panic mode, thinking the worst.

"I want to see my sister; she was admitted here."

"What's her name," the nurse at the reception area brightly asked with a smile pasted on her face. For someone who had been on night duty, she looked fresh and full of energy that PJ was failing to muster at the moment.

"Edwina James."

The nurse quickly typed the name into the computer and looked up to PJ with a frown.

"Are you sure she was admitted here Miss, coz there isn't any record."

"Edwina said City Hospital, private wing when she called. She's definitely here."

The nurse retyped again and stood up from her chair, "I am sorry you must have got the wrong information, there is no Edwina James in our records. Maybe she was admitted to another hospital."

PJ was already impatiently tapping her foot on the floor. "I swear she called from here," she insisted. She took out her phone, "Isn't this the hospital phone number."

The nurse opened her eyes widely and shook her head, "It's ours but we don't have an Edwina here."

A doctor came into the reception area. "Is there a problem nurse Philips?" he asked.

"Hi Doctor, I am Peggy James. I received a call from my sister some thirty minutes back and she told me she was here."

The doctor frowned and Peggy already knew what he was about to say.

She raised her hand to stop him. "My sister sounded weak and scared."

"I am sorry miss but I didn't attend to a patient by that name."

"Isn't there another doctor who attended to her then," PJ asked.

"Hey Miss," both the doctor and nurse shouted in unison when PJ started walking towards the wards seeing that they wouldn't assist her in any way but pretend that nothing was amiss.

"You are not meant to go there," they said while she snorted and dashed to a nearby door and she could hear their feet rushing towards her.

"Step mother," she said in shock as her step mother abruptly stood up from a chair when she rushed for the nearest door and got in. Apparently, she had got into the right room after all. "Miss," the doctor called.

Her step mother spoke up, "It's fine doctor Anderson. She's, my daughter."

The doctor nodded and shut the door.

"What's going on?"

Edwina's eyes were shut and she was lying on the bed with a drip on her hand and bandages on her wrists.

Her step mother seemed exhausted too, with no make-up on her face. That was a first; considering her step mother always made sure she looked great, even if she was just stepping out of the house to grab the morning paper.

"Why all the secrecy. The nurse and that doctor told me that Edwina wasn't here."

"It's because I asked them to," her step mother answered before she slumped back on the chair.

"I didn't want Henry to find out about it. Does he know that you came to the hospital?" PJ shook her head. Of all things her step mother should be concerned about; it was Edwina not about her dad finding out. The man loved his daughters and of course he might want to be kept in the loop.

At assessing the situation, PJ knew she should have told her dad about it after all.

"What do you want?"

PJ was left stunned. "Edwina is my young sister, that's why I rushed here when she called. What's going on?"

"PJ" Edwina weakly called and opened her eyes. PJ rushed to her bed side. "Hey sweetie what's going on, why are you here."

A flicker of fear passed through her eyes that had Edwina clutching at her arm before she stared at her mother. "Please don't let her hurt me," she whispered weakly.

She appeared to gain more strength as she clutched PJs arm when the doctor and nurse got into the ward.

"Edwina, stop being silly. We are here to help you," her mother said as she screamed and three orderlies dressed in their white uniforms came in to hold her down. Adele pulled PJ from her while Edwina's screams grew louder and the doctor injected her with a sedative.

"She is a liar, don't listen to her," Edwina said weakly as her eyes began to shut down, drowsy from the drug.

"What's going on here?" PJ forcefully asked this time, shocked at what she had just witnessed. Her step mother ignored her but addressed the doctor. "May we use your office for a chat?" The doctor cleared his throat and nodded.

"Let's go and talk in private," her step mother advised before she walked out of the ward. PJ followed her. Once they were in the office and alone, her step mother advised, "Take a seat." PJ shook her head.

She preferred standing. Her stepmother nodded before she settled down and crossed her legs. "Edwina tried to take her own life."

PJ gasped. "How and why?"

"She slit her wrists. I found her having passed out from the loss of blood on the bathroom floor two days ago."

PJ settled down on the chair she had been offered prior. "Did she mention why she did it once she woke up."

"I know why she did it. I found her pregnancy test under the bed. She is expecting. When I confronted her, she confirmed it? After she told me who the pregnancy was for, I knew they would not be a good future for her, so I told her we had to get rid of it. That's when she started screaming and accusing me of being unfeeling." Adele scoffed at that. "Of all things my daughter thinks I am a horrible monster when she is the one who went after a married man."

By the time she finished PJ was left stunned, this couldn't be true. The Edwina she knew wouldn't hurt anyone like that and on top of that she would never pursue such a relationship.

They might have had their own share of ups and downs as siblings, but Edwina, no, she wouldn't, PJ thought. She had always hoped that her young sister would take after their father more and this time when PJ came back from the States, her young sister had been rather accommodative.

"This can't be right," PJ finally said. Her step mother snorted. "You are being naïve like your young sister."

"Ok so if she is pregnant and wants to keep the child, what's wrong with that?"

Her step mother laughed. "Are you joshing me right now? Don't you know how our society treats single mothers and to top it all, she had to fall pregnant for that man! He will not let her live. She thinks she is safe if he finds out but she won't be."

"Who is the man, stepmother?"

Her step mother slumped on the chair in defeat before she muttered, "the king."

"No, this is not right," PJ abruptly stood up from the chair. This had to be the lie that Edwina was speaking about. Her step mother snorted. "Ask her when she's awake. She thinks he loves her and he would leave the queen for her. I wonder how I raised such a silly girl. I know I usually tell her to aim high but I didn't expect she would do this."

"No, no, this can't be right," PJ said, no longer listening to her stepmother. She walked out of the office. This was a lie. This was the King that her step mother was loosely slandering and her future father-in-law. Edwina used to say Chad was way older and ancient in her eyes, what more his dad?

She wasn't aware of how long she stayed at the park afterwards, wandering aimlessly. Her phone rang. Her step mother had been calling nonstop but she wasn't willing to listen to anymore of her lies.

She looked at the screen and noticed it was Chad.

"Hey baby" he greeted her in his deep voice as PJ clasped the phone for comfort.

"Hi honey, how are you?"

"Good, I miss you love," Chad said and PJ could feel a trickle of a tear fall on her face, she dabbed on her face with the palm of her hand. *This is all messed up,* she thought. No, she had to verify with Edwina once she woke up if it was true.

"How's Gerard and everyone," PJ asked while she savagely brushed off the tears that had now increased.

"Everyone is doing just great. The reason why I called is to inform you that I have to go away for a while. There has been a new development."

"Ok" PJ replied.

"Wow woman, I expected for you to throw a tantrum," Chad said and PJ could imagine him smiling while he said that.

"Is something the matter hon?"

"Nothing, I'm just feeling under the weather that's all."

"Ooh, love, wish I was there with you. Are you experiencing any morning sickness?"

PJ clutched at her tummy. "I am not."

"When I come back, we will get married as soon as possible, you hear me."

She chuckled a bit. "Aye, aye captain," she whispered before Chad told her he loved her and hung up. She stood up from the park bench. It was time she spoke with her young sister and cleared out this mess before she spoke to her dad.

• • ❦ • •

"HEY PJ," EDWINA GREETED when she got into the ward. She looked well rested and not the frantic and panicked person she was a few hours back. Her stepmother was nowhere to be seen.

"Bought you your favorite," PJ said and handed her the box of pizza.

"I guess I should get sick more often," Edwina said with a chuckle before she took a bite at the pizza. PJ tentatively sat on the bed and curiously looked at her. "Edwina what's going on?" she finally asked.

Edwina pushed the box aside at the question and sadly looked at her hands.

PJ reached towards them, "Why did you hurt yourself?"

Edwina looked up and pasted a brave smile.

"I would rather die along with the child, than to let her do that. Thank you. I don't know what you said to convince mom, but she promised that she would not try to get rid of the pregnancy."

"Was she right about who the pregnancy is for?" PJ asked.

"If she told you, it was a married man, she was lying." At that, PJ heaved a long sigh, relieved that her step mother had pulled one over her.

"They live separate lives, and their being together is for society's sake."

PJ's eyes widened. "What are you saying, Edwina, who is the father of the child?" At the answers her young sister was giving, PJ had a tight and sickening feeling in the pit of her stomach.

Her young sister smiled innocently. "Terry off course, Terry Jonson, the king."

PJ nearly fainted on the spot and sat there in a daze not believing what her sister had told her. "He is our father's age, Edwina and how is it possible?"

Edwina laughed. "We fell in love; it's as simple as that PJ. Mom thinks if he were to find out he would kill me, but it's not true. He is devoted and he loves me."

"No Edwina, no," PJ muttered under her breath, feeling like one having a nightmare that was failing to end.

"How do you think I knew about your relationship with Chad? Terry told me. I knew about it, way before you came back and I had to pretend. Pretending is what I have been doing throughout ever since you came back. It's so funny how you forget who I truly am and try to mold me into a good girl."

Something happened as she spoke; she sat upright on the bed and smiled, this time giving her a smug look that PJ knew so well. That triumphant smile that Edwina could pull when they were growing up after PJ got in trouble because of her. The smug smile that made PJ hate coming back to Safe Haven and prefer being in a foreign land even after she turned eighteen and was no longer under her mother's guardianship but considered an adult.

The same look that Adele had when PJ and her mother boarded the plane twelve years ago. Proud and cold. "Terry will marry me, don't worry about it," she announced while PJ cradled her head in her hands finally believing her.

"O God Edwina, what have you done?" She said and clamped her hand over her mouth.

"Unlike you I know what I want. By the way, if you think of saying anything to that boyfriend of yours or dad, you have to think twice because I know that you are pregnant. Just one word and everything will come out in the open. Imagine how it will go. The criticism and what about dad. Heart attack on the way, because his favorite daughter turned out to be a harlot."

PJ gasped in shock. The door opened. "Oh good, I see you are much better and you girls had time to have your little chat," Adele said with a smile.

"I can't... I can't be here, I have to go," PJ raised her hand in surrender and stood up.

"Before you go, we need to talk, since you convinced me that Edwina should keep the pregnancy."

PJ nodded and rushed to the door, she had really thought Edwina had changed and was not taking after Adele. How wrong she had been. She could hear both mother and daughter laughing behind her back.

"Mother," Edwina looked at her with a raised brow. "What do you want to talk about with PJ?"

"Nothing to bother your pretty head over. If it's the throne you want, that's what you will get. Trust me. Let me leave and talk to that girl in case she rushes to her father and blurts out everything to him. The news might shock him and I still need him around."

She winked, blew a couple of kisses and followed PJ to the car.

· · ✿ · ·

"SWEET PEA IS SOMETHING bothering you," PJ's father asked her over the dinner table.

"Nothing, I am fine," she answered. She had been toying around with the food in her plate and going over what her step mother had said in the car. She advised PJ to give up on Chad and persuade him to marry her young sister instead.

PJ suspected she had received more shocks in one day than she could ever encounter in a lifetime.

Her step mother was worried over the king getting rid of Edwina once he found out about the baby, while Edwina kept on insisting that the King loved her and he no longer wanted the queen as his wife.

PJ was yet to break the news to her father pertaining to Chad's proposal. Everything was such a mess.

She had crossed her arms over her breast in the car when her step mother had told her what she could do to save her young sister from herself, while PJ resolutely told her step mother that it was impossible.

"Chad and I love each other. You can't expect me to tell him to marry Edwina."

"You are not like your mother at all. You are a cold person," her step mother had sneeringly remarked.

"What do you mean by that? Are you saying I should let you and your daughter walk over me like you did with my mother to the point she left for the States?"

"Now there it is," her step mother pointed to her. "The vindictive PJ that Henry fails to see bent on ruining me and my daughter all because your father loved me instead of your mother. Is this your revenge then?"

The woman was twisting her words and she wasn't going to listen to her anymore. PJ had slumped back on the seat instead, her mouth thinned in anger while she resolutely looked out of the car window.

Once they got home, she had rushed to her room and locked herself in it, until she was called for supper by one of the maids.

Her father nodded and continued on with the meal, satisfied with her answer that nothing was wrong.

She stared at him and for the first time felt anger towards him. What he put her and her mother through. None of what was taking place now could have happened if only he had stood his ground and married the woman of his choice.

Instead, he let his parents arrange a marriage for him while he was in love with someone else. Got married to her and still continued on with a relationship with his lover.

Did he even realize how her world suddenly changed because of his actions? At the age of twelve, she had to leave everything she knew and start over. Once her mother found out about the affair, she couldn't bear it. To top it all, PJ could well remember the satisfied smirk that had been on Adele's face when she spotted them boarding the plane.

PJ didn't understand some of the things that were happening until she was old enough, but that smug expression, she still couldn't get it off her mind.

She was able to visit Safe Haven afterwards but her home no longer felt the same. Her new step mother had taken charge of everything and that included sacking everyone who had worked at the house when her mother was in residence. PJ was now around strangers and the one-month holidays used to be torture to her young mind and soul. She didn't fit in at home and she didn't fit in, in the foreign land.

Strangers were in her home in Safe Haven including a young sister who hated her, while in the States she was bullied and the other kids made fun of her accent and the way she dressed. That's how she met Barb. A bubbly girl two years her senior who didn't care much about what people thought about her.

Her mother, having taken note of her loneliness too, had invited Sharon, a childhood friend to stay with them in the States. The parents were rather thrilled at the opportunity and easily gave permission for their daughter to study abroad.

PJ missed Shaz friendship at times, but her betrayal still hurt because she had never imagined for a second that she would do that to her.

"When is Edwina coming back?" her father asked her step mother and continued with his meal.

"Darling, Edwina said she was having a blast with her friends, so she was contemplating coming back next week."

PJ abruptly stood up from the chair. She was failing to stomach the pretentious people around her. "I am tired, I'll retire early." she nodded to both of them. "Good night."

She walked out of the dining room with one thought in mind. Tomorrow she will go to her granny's place. At the same time, she hoped whatever Chad had been tasked to do, would be completed early before all hell broke loose.

Chapter 20

PJ woke up to the sound of someone loudly knocking on her door. "Who is it?" she shouted and abruptly rose from bed to rush to the loo. She gagged and after she was done, felt drained. "PJ ma'am" the maid called as she got into her room. She knocked on the bathroom door, "Are you okay?"

PJ gurgled and spit out the water before she replied, "I will be out in a minute."

"Your father urgently requires your presence in the living room," the maid advised before she left the room.

"And then," another maid who had been waiting for her friend outside the door asked. "The news must be true; she was throwing up in the bathroom."

The second maid gasped, "It can't be true, and Miss PJ is too sweet of a girl to be what was being said in the paper." Her friend scoffed, "we are yet to see that, but right now the father is breathing fire," she giggled as she rushed for the living room where she would pretend to be cleaning so she saw the show about to happen.

PJ shut her eyes and splashed water on her face. Once she felt better, she straightened up, rushed to her room to put on a robe before she went downstairs, wondering what could have happened for her father to summon her early in the morning.

"What is this," her father yelled at her as he threw the daily paper in her face when she got into the living room. He had been pacing up and down while her step mother was insisting that he take it easy.

"Dad, what is going on," PJ asked and looked at the front page. There pasted for all to see was the worst headline ever.

Miss Peggy James, Mistress to Prince Chadwick Johnson is expecting a love child with her former American lover Tony Clark.

She stared at her step mother and raised her voice accusingly at her, "These are lies, and you did this!"

The sound of a slap was heard as PJ clutched at her stinging cheek, she tried to make sense of what was happening because for a brief moment she was disoriented and looked in horror at her father who was panting heavily, after having slapped her.

"How dare you accuse my wife over such nonsense?"

"Daddy I swear these are all lies," she frantically said as tears fell from her eyes.

"Lies, hmmm and you accuse my wife of doing this?"

Her father snorted and raised his hand again while she flinched. "You haven't changed at all. You still lie all the time, how could you. What will people say pertaining to this? Is this what your mother taught you?"

PJ curled her hands on the side, not believing her dad could slander her mother like that. "My mother brought me up the best way she could."

"As a harlot," her father bellowed while she gasped in shock.

"So which part is not true? Are you or are you not pregnant?"

PJ opened her mouth and snapped it shut. "Henry, take it easy, you will raise your blood pressure over nothing."

Her father ignored her step mother but continued looking at her. His eyes had reddened and she could see the veins popping from his forehead while he tried to control his breathing.

"Answer me!" he bellowed and PJ yelped then knelt down. "I'm sorry papa," she wailed. "I am pregnant, it's true, but I swear this is Chad's baby."

Silence followed as she stared on the ground and tears continued falling.

"Get out!"

She looked up as if he had physically struck her again. "Get out of my house and get out of the country. Go back to the states and never come back. From today onwards, you are not my daughter..."

"Henry," her step mother said pleadingly, "Don't do this,"

He grunted and still looked to his daughter disappointment etched on his face, "I can never harbor a harlot in my own home."

"Dad," PJ wailed. He forcefully helped her stand and pushed her away. "Out!"

PJ looked at her sire and knew she wouldn't reason with him, especially in his state. She turned and started walking away at the same time her heart breaking into a million pieces while she wailed. The sound of a dull thud and her step mother screaming had her turning back. She screamed and rushed to her father who had collapsed on the floor.

• • ❦ • •

"NO, NO, NO" ADELE YELLED when she saw PJ and her grandmother walking towards her. "Your witch of a granddaughter cannot be here. Henry will surely die."

Henry's mother looked at her with disdain in her eyes before she sternly said, "Stop trying to cause drama here. PJ is Henry's daughter and she has as much right as you to be here. I will hear nothing of the accusations."

Adele snapped shut her mouth and huffed. The old woman must have used her resources and connections as usual because no one was there to witness her drama. The press that had been there before when all the confusion had started in the morning was nowhere to be seen.

Henry was still in ICU as his daughter had acted fast once he fell and called an ambulance. The old man appeared to still be holding on to dear life despite finding out what his favorite daughter was capable of.

She coughed and feigned being the hurt wife.

"It seems you still do not care about your son's well-being, that's why you insist on her being here."

"Adele," the old woman looked at her threateningly. "Be Careful of what you are about to say or else I will reveal your true colors to the world. You are my son's worst mistake and it's not PJ who caused this but you."

"How could you accuse me of such a thing, old lady," she snapped while a doctor approached them. "Ladies, ladies please less noise, you are in a hospital."

"PJ, are you okay?" her grandmother turned to her and helped her settle down, while Adele scoffed.

"How can she be okay when she is carrying a bastard and the daddy isn't known?"

PJ sharply inhaled and excused herself on that note before she rushed to the loo where she gagged.

No matter the self-comforting words she had said to herself a million times, she still felt this was all her fault. Her father was lying in bed, fighting for his life all because of her.

"Chad where are you; I need you," she mumbled after she threw up the last of the meal her granny had forcefully made her eat.

She was shaken to the core. The reporters had swarmed on her, questions coming from all ends after the ambulance had taken her father to the hospital. If it weren't for Morgan, Chad's head of security, arriving and swooping her away from the crowd that had surrounded her outside her home, she doesn't know what would have become of her. Morgan is the one who called her granny and updated her on what was happening. He had assured her that Chad would be arriving soon.

• • ⁂ • •

TWO DAYS LATER.

PJ looked to the last people who had come for the funeral, walking away. Her grandmother had informed her that she would find her in the car. The king and queen had paid their last respect before they left. Her grandmother with the help of the king had made sure that everything was kept private even though Adele had tried to create another scene over PJ not attending the funeral.

"Papa, I am sorry," PJ finally broke down and wept. She had been numb for the past two day after the doctor informed the family that her dad hadn't made it. Not a tear was shed from her eyes. Edwina, like her mother, had been quick to hurl insults at her once she arrived at the hospital, looking like one coming from a vacation.

She wasn't aware of how long she sat in the grass near her father's newly turned grave which was next to her mother's. All of a sudden, she was engulfed in a warm hug as she sniffed the spicy musky scent she always liked. "Chad," she whispered and huddled deeply into the embrace, weeping over what could have been.

"Sorry baby I came late," he whispered as his voice cracked a bit. For two days she had not been able to sleep, overcome with grief. Finally, the exhausting took over as her head remained on his chest and she shut her eyes.

Chad stood up holding her so she wouldn't topple on the ground before he swiftly picked her up. He brushed aside a lock of her braid and nearly groaned, damning the weather elements for delaying his flight back home. He should have been with her all along. In the week he hadn't seen her, she appeared to have lost weight. He sighed and walked towards the car.

• • ⚜ • •

"YOU WILL MARRY THE young sister or any of the other girls but not Peggy James," the King said. Chad looked at his father in disbelief.

He was in the study; passing out what he thought was the best solution for everyone concerned. It was a week after Chad had come back from investigating some of the ministers who worked with his father. A week after PJ's father passed on and a week of her staying in the palace, right next to him despite the King's disapproval. Chad realized that his love went deep for PJ, especially after meeting the man who was one of the key players in what was happening in her life.

"I respect your decision my King, but that doesn't mean I will follow it. PJ is my love and I will marry only her."

His father snorted, "So you are willing to put our family honor on the line because of that loose girl."

Chad coldly looked at his father, "She is not loose and that child she is carrying is mine. I will not let society dictate to us how we should live. If my being here will tarnish your noble name then I will leave. After all I never wanted any of this." He pointed to everything surrounding him.

A gasp was heard as his mother got into the study. "Don't tell me you are still fighting over Chad and his girlfriend."

"Martha, reason with him."

His wife shook her head. "I am on his side, Terry. If he wants to marry her, it's his choice. It's not like any of the people passing bad comments will have to live with PJ. They don't know that girl and what she has been through to judge her like that. If Chad says she is expecting his child, there is no reason to doubt that."

"Martha, you are so naive like your son. A bastard will end up taking the throne and all because you believed your son. He is in love with her and he can't see clearly. I am the King on the other hand and such a scandal will put everything that my family has strived for in jeopardy."

"What scandal" his wife raised a brow in question while he groaned. Of course, she had to go behind his back like his son and the grandmother to clear that girl's name.

In a week they had managed to silence the shady press as they used the reputable ones to set the record straight. Chad proudly went around with PJ everywhere as he had been doing ever since she came to Safe Haven.

Everyone in his life wasn't being reasonable, the King thought. They acted like nothing was amiss.

He wearily sighed and groaned. He couldn't let Chadwick's threat slide as he knew his son was capable of leaving everything behind.

Meghan had left the palace and all its luxury to be married to a simple cop in the States and she even accepted being exiled from her own family without breaking a sweat. He groaned again and wondered what these kids of nowadays prioritized. When he was growing up, children listened to their parents and did what they were told, not this new thought and streak of independence that was slowly seeping through his kingdom.

Had he been wrong in sending all his children to a foreign land so that they received the best education they possibly could? Michael appeared to be well settled, having come back immediately after school while Chad the crown prince decided to stay back.

As a father, he had thought once he turned thirty the boy would come around, but now with PJ in the mix, he doubted it.

"Just fix a private ceremony and use a few of the notable press to cover the event," he resignedly said. His wife smiled and hugged him when he said that while he chuckled as his son suddenly breathed a sigh of relief. So, he did love his people after all, maybe there was still hope then.

"This is the last favor that I will do for you, since you helped in identifying the corrupt ministers in my circle. But I am a King and what my people want comes first before everything else. I do what's best for Safe Haven."

"Thank you, father," Chad nodded and left the study.

Epilogue

"HEY," Chad tilted PJ's chin up with his finger, "It's all going to be ok." She nodded and returned to that warm hug as they swayed to the beat of the music.

"About the honeymoon."

That statement had her looking up with accusation in her eyes while he chuckled. The queen, her grandmother, uncle, aunt and friends had convinced PJ that this was the right thing to do, when all she had wanted was to mourn for her father and for them to leave her alone.

They had hounded her like crazy with implied bribes and threats from her grandmother and best friend Barb while the rest smothered her with love. Somehow, they convinced the King too and here she was at her wedding reception and not happy about having to pretend that all was well. The peals of accusation that her step mother had thrown her way, still echoed in her ears while her father's disappointed expression was still etched on her mind.

Chad had given her the space she needed at the same time stayed near her for when she needed him ever since he came back. Her uncle had flown in for the funeral including Barb, hence with all people who mattered around, they had been able to pull the small function without a hitch, whilst she still battled with herself over what had happened in just a month.

A giggle was heard, as PJ turned to look at Meghan who also came in for the wedding. For this once, the King appeared to have let her back into the kingdom. Chad's family appeared to have drama like hers. Drama she has always managed to avoid by being in a foreign land.

Now she was back and she just had that anxious feeling in the pit in her stomach that it wasn't over yet.

Barb as usual had glossed over the fact that only a few found the love of their life like her. Silly Barb, she even patted herself for the fact that she had made PJ go out with her to the club that night.

"Like I said, a rich man and that's what you managed to get. When you leave him darling, do make sure that you get the mansion so we can weep together in it. When he leaves you, take the kingdom along with you."

PJ had screamed and hurled a pillow at her for saying that. Barb had made the statement the day before while they had her small bachelorette party, with Meghan dancing like crazy to nonexistent music. She was just happy to be back.

Slowly but gradually PJ in a month had learnt to accept what had happened and with Chad's support, her family and his family, she was beginning to smile a little too.

"How can you think about a honeymoon when I am still in this state?"

"What state honey, the pregnant one."

He winked when she tried to step on his foot. "My dear wife, I am not having wicked thoughts. I just wanted to inform you that we will be leaving for the States along with Meghan and your uncle for three months, until everything dies down completely, that's when we will come back."

PJ breathed in sharply and looked at her husband. He had thought of everything. A tear slid down her face that he managed to catch with his finger and frown.

"Honey I still haven't figured out what your tears mean. One moment you look like one about to murder me and the next with tenderness like am a hero. Which is which, am I a villain or hero."

PJ chuckled and clamped her mouth shut at the realization that she had laughed loudly as her uncle who was dancing with her aunt, grinned and winked their way.

"That's what I want to hear," her husband commented. "That laugh that makes me crazy." At seeing the love in his eyes, she felt that all was going to be well and she was just being paranoid over nothing. She smiled and cradled his face. "I love you, she whispered before he kissed her and she kissed him back with all the love and passion she felt, as that kiss thawed all the numb emotions and suddenly brought them to life again.

A flash and shutter of a camera sounded as the camera man looked at the picture of the beautiful couple on the dance floor and grinned, "Perfect," he said, having made up his mind on the picture to use for the article he was meant to write. An article that will no doubt put the haters to shame once and for all.

• • ⁘ • •

A DAY AFTER THE WEDDING

ADELE looked in horror at the article on the front page of the newspaper before she furiously crumpled it in her hands and shoved it with the tea set on the coffee table to the floor, while screaming out her frustrations as she did so. The servants rushed to the door after hearing the scream and sound of pottery crushing down. They found the madam of the house pacing up and down in the living room, looking crazed and furious all at the same time.

"This is not the result I want," she yelled and cracked her knuckles while still pacing the room.

"No!" Adele yelled and pulled at her hair. The article had been short and straight to the point. Nothing was mentioned about the scandal that had taken place a month ago. According to the article, the prince had married the love of his life in a beautiful private ceremony, surrounded with close family and friends since the bride was still in mourning over her father's death.

The journalist had glossed over the couple's intense love for each and how they looked forward to starting a family. Adele snorted over that note. Everyone appeared to have made an exception about PJ's condition and the fact that she might not be carrying the prince's child but her lovers.

Countless years of plotting her revenge and that's what she got? A happily ever after? What happened to the society that had been quick to cast her aside like a scarlet woman? The society that still looked down on her like she was the scum of the earth.

Why hadn't they done the same thing to PJ? Ostracized PJ like they did to her? Blamed her for being a loose woman. Isn't that what society was good at? Always blaming the woman.

Instead from that article it appeared that they would be willing to accept PJ whole heartedly into their midst.

This isn't the end; she thought to herself and shook her head, looking resolutely outside the window and oblivious of the maid clearing the tea things.

Retribution is what she was going to get for the years she silently suffered from the hands of PJ and her virtuous mother. Even after they left Safe Haven, people had deemed them victims when it was the other way round.

She was the victim in all this. She knew Henry before his parents arranged for him to get married to Ellen. Sweet, innocent Ellen, who had been clueless over what her new husband was up to.

Ellen took Henry away from her by simply being her. Kind, beautiful and charitable. Henry, who used to make promises to her that he felt nothing for Ellen, had betrayed her in the worst possible way by falling in love with his arranged bride.

The day PJ was born, he was ready to leave her, claiming he wanted to be there for his daughter and to be a great role model for her. Henry was campaigning to be the father of the year for his daughter but never did he think about what that decision of his would cost her.

Her name had already been tarnished; her family gave up on her because she had persisted in pursuing a relationship with someone who wasn't of her class. Whose family looked down upon her and insulted her family's upbringing and members every time they had the opportunity to do so.

She had lost her youth and chances of getting married to a good man, so she wasn't going out without a fight. Adele sought the help of the traditional healers to keep Henry with her and for a while was happy. Despite being warned that he might not be the same man but one who she could control and manipulate hence his love wouldn't be the same, she had gone ahead to feed him the love portion with his meal.

She was content as long as Henry came back to her. Manipulating and controlling him might work to her advantage too. What did the traditional healers know anyway, and why would they judge her? They manipulated people for a living.

Henry had returned to his usual dotting self and she decided to give him a child, to keep him by her side for good. Such was her shock when she discovered Ellen was expecting too. A second child while all the time she had thought the medicine had worked and the man wasn't sleeping with his wife.

Things did turn around for the best and luck appeared to be on her side because Ellen gave birth to a still born baby. For four more years Adele bided her time and finally appeared in front of Ellen with Edwina, a reminder of the child she lost.

Henry had complained that Ellen had never been the same after the loss of their second child; hence Edwina was Adele's saving grace and proof of Henry's infidelity. Once Ellen found out there was a child, especially one born during the same period she lost her second child, she couldn't get over the betrayal and left.

And now her daughter was back, living her life and happy like her mother had been once upon a time. Adele scoffed. She could still make her life miserable despite what the press had said. She grinned at the thought of the ace up her sleeve that she would use. This wasn't over until she said so. Henry had died too early before he felt the pain and loss; she had to endure in the twenty-six years with him.

Ellen and Henry were gone but their daughter would get the brunt of it and she would make sure of that. No palace walls would stop what was soon to come.

. . ⚘ . .

THANK YOU FOR READING *The Prince's Bride.* I hope you enjoyed Chad and PJ's story and I would appreciate it if you let me know what you thought by leaving a review.

NOTE FROM AUTHOR

When I sat down to write about the prince's bride, I was still debating on how my story should continue after their first meeting. I have made a lot of changes in this book from the initial thought and I love the outcome. Therefore, I left some things hanging since I might write part two to this story in the future, with Chad and PJ appearing briefly while I tie up the loose ends pertaining to Edwina and her mother.

ALL BOOKS BY YVONNE SIBANDA

FAMILY MATTERS SERIES
The Inconvenient Marriage
Finding a husband for Cissy
A Risky Venture
PERFECT GENTLEMAN SERIES
The Perfect Gentleman
The Designer's Wicked Intentions
NEXT GENERATION SERIES
Sweet Crazy Love
Loving a Compton
ARRANGED MARRIAGES
The Pastor's Wife
The Wrong Couple

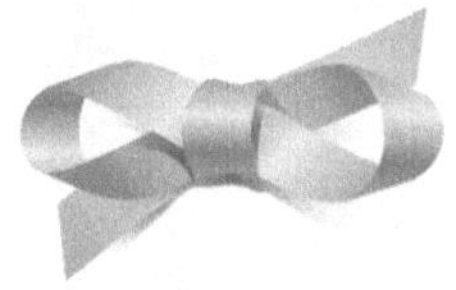

ABOUT YVONNE SIBANDA

Writing has always been my passion from as long as I can remember. Romance stories are my forte as I think that each and every one of us is affected by matters of the heart. I hope that everyone who grabs hold of any of my books enjoys reading them and much as I enjoy writing them. I live and work out of my home in a small mining town of Hwange and you will notice that I appear to like stories with small towns in my books too. With a well-knit and close community that knows who is who.

WHERE TO FIND YVONNE

Facebook https://www.facebook.com/vovosibbs/

Once in a while I drop a cover image of my latest books I am working on and also an update for my books that will be out. If there are any promotions running on some of the sites where I publish my books, I also drop in the information and link so you can easily use those to your advantage.

WordPress https://yvonnesbooks.wordpress.com

I have a website where you can also read some of my work, including short stories I might have written in between my long length novels.

Thank you again for your support and for those who continue helping me in this journey. To God the Father, Son and the Holy Spirit, may your name be forever glorified. Amen.